SEBASTIAN CARMICHAEL

GARY SEEARY

-GS-

Sebastian Carmichael
Gary Seeary

First published 2015
This edition published 2017 by Gary Seeary Books

Email: seearygj@gmail.com or visit www.seearygj.wixsite

Copyright © Gary Seeary

All rights reserved. No part of this printed or video publication may be reproduced, stored in or introduced into a retrieval system, or transmitted, in any form, or by any means (electrical, mechanical, photocopying, recording or otherwise) without the prior written permission of the publisher and copyright owner.

Designer / typesetter: Working Type Studio (www.workingtype.com.au)
Printed in Melbourne by Lightning Source Australia

This is a work of fiction. Names, characters, businesses, places, events and incidents are either the products of the author's imagination or used in a fictitious manner. King's College is a fictitious college within Melbourne University and not an actual part of the university at any time. Any resemblance to actual persons, living or dead is purely coincidental.

National Library of Australia Cataloguing-in-Publication entry
Seeary, Gary, 1958- author
Sebastian Carmichael
ISBN: 9780648002826 (Paperback)
ISBN: 9780648002833 (E-book)
Fiction Australian participation in Spanish Civil War
Dewey Decimal Classification notation: 823.4

Also by Gary Seeary:
The Beautiful Journey

Their Peace

Now peace has come, but they that fell
Know only that they sought it well.
They cannot know that peace has come
Let us make haste and let us build
Great worlds with strength
And wonder filled,
Then shall they know their
Peace has come.

—Nettie Palmer

To our parents

Contents

1

The Magenta Push

The second after I had turned a sharp left into Lygon Street I knew it was a huge mistake.

Bugger! I was already late and now these blokes.

Two members of the Push from the Magenta Club were standing in the middle of the footpath at the entrance to Magenta Lane.

The boys from the Push were real hard nuts. Luckily for everyone in this part of Carlton they usually stayed at the bottom of their lane like a pack of faithful guard dogs, casting a wary eye over the regular procession of men looking for the female favours that their establishment provided.

The local male population mustn't have had too many itches to scratch this night for two of the Push to be out on Lygon Street.

These blokes — one big, the other little — strutted about like prize peacocks while they knocked around some poor drunken sod who nearly lost his precious bottle, before they helped him on his way with a solid shove in the back.

Once they'd seen me, I knew I was in for it.

I thought for a second about making a dash across the road, until I remembered what my dad told me not long before I moved down to the city six months ago.

If you walk away once, they'll always have you pegged as a chicken. Do you want that?

Great advice, however, I could never recall my dad testing his theory by going for a walk around Carlton after dark. When he did come to the city for a rare visit to his sister, my Aunty May, he only ever walked from her boarding house to the pub on the corner.

Even though I'd stayed with my aunt several times during school holidays when I was younger, it wasn't until I'd moved down to board with her that I realised how much of a fish out of water I really was, floundering about for several months before I began to cotton on to how things were done around here. Whether they were Irish, Jewish or Italian, every community had a survival plan, which included looking after their own. I learned quickly not to trifle with the locals.

I didn't have much of a plan for these Magenta blokes though, trifle or otherwise. I kept walking straight ahead, feigning a wave to a non-existent friend on the other side of Lygon Street in a poor attempt to bluff my way through. I knew it wasn't going to work.

"Hey you, boyo," squeaked an Irish voice from the smaller of the two. "I wanna' talk to you."

I tried to sidestep him, but he was wide awake to that and shot out a heavy black boot just in time to catch me clean on the left ankle.

"Jesus!" I screamed out, hopping around on one foot, my ankle in searing pain. "What the bloody hell are ya doin'?"

The little Irishman stepped up close to my face. "Now, boyo, I don't wanna hear you goin' around, using the Lord's name in vain, or else, I'll box your bloody ears in. Got it?"

His massive mate stepped behind me to put me in a full headlock, which was standard practice for mugs like these. I struggled but there was no way I could break free of this big galoot. He was as strong as an ox and almost lifted me off the ground.

"Oh, my Lord," the big man choked out, in a strong cockney accent. "He stinks like a thousand sheep, Ryan."

"Here, you take him," the big Englishman whined, pushing me back towards his little 'Mick' mate.

"I don't want the stinkin' eejit," yelled back the Irishman, pushing me in-between them again, both men having a good chuckle over their silly game.

"You'd be from Gennons then, wouldn't ya?" the big Pommy git asked in a friendlier tone.

I didn't answer him back, firstly because I was too shit scared, and also because my thoughts kept racing back to how late I was going to be for a special dinner at my aunt's.

"Listen, and listen careful, boyo," demanded the Irishman poking me in the chest. "Some of the girls on Queensberry reckon they've been accosted lately by a young turd that stinks like a sheep ... and you fit the bill perfectly."

"All right, before you start sayin' there's a dozen tanneries off Queensberry, I'm bettin' you're the one who would take a free piece of pie if you could get away with it. So, I'm suggesting you keep giving it to your mummy and leave our girls alone."

Now, they had my attention the smart bastards. They could've just given me a clip under the ear, and then sent me on my way. But no, they had to bring my mum into it, which was the wrong thing to do.

"Yeah, I think I know the fella you're talkin' about. He works at Gennons as a puller, down the other end of the shop. Always talkin' about tryin' to pick up sheilas on Queensberry, giving 'em plenty of lip, that sort of shit. I can't remember his name off-hand ... hang on a sec. I've got it!"

The little 'Mick' leant forward to hear what I had to say ... *Bang!*

I copped him, smack on his left ear with a huge haymaking right.

He was still doing a full pirouette, while holding his ear and swearing his lungs out by the time I made it halfway to Argyle Square. At the corner I took a peek behind, only to see the big Pom hammering after me. I bolted, flat out, diagonally across the Square, almost cleaning up a young couple pushing a large Landau pram. I didn't need to turn around again, because I knew he would keep coming.

Hell! I might have smashed that poor Irish sod's ear-drum.

I flew through the barely ajar wrought iron gates at the entrance to the Women's Hospital, running almost blindly between the old and new buildings, until I reached a car park in the grounds at the far end of Faraday Street. Luckily, there was a thick hedge on the outside, large enough for me to slip in the middle of, giving me a reprieve to catch my breath. From there, lit up like Christmas, I could see the whole area clearly from Melbourne University to the end of Faraday Street.

It had to be well after nine o'clock by now and I knew my aunt would be having kittens waiting up for me. She was on the edge at the best of times.

After ten minutes, I thought I might have seen the Pom stalking around somewhere in the vicinity, frustrated that he couldn't find the little turd that gave his mate an earful. I guess even these Magenta mugs would eventually twig that I didn't work at Gennons but that didn't mean they'd give up looking for me in every tannery, until they found me at Cooks.

Twenty minutes later I hadn't seen anyone on the streets, except a couple of university students walking up towards their college. So I thought it might be worth a shot to head north towards the cemetery and then back-track all the way down Rathdowne Street, where I would be as good as home.

I stayed on the opposite side of the road to the university, trying to keep out of as much streetlight as possible. I walked backwards for a while, making sure my new Pommy mate didn't sneak up on me from behind. As I turned around, I saw a large figure coming out of a side-street a hundred yards ahead where the road started to curve. It appeared to be a man, but I couldn't be sure, beginning to doubt myself as my eyes started to play tricks.

As the figure neared a streetlight, I could see it was lifting its feet to pick up speed. It was the Pom and he was running straight at me.

I ran out onto Swanston Street, without even looking to see if there were any cars coming or not. I just wanted to get as far away from this big bastard as possible. Even though I was panicking, I knew I couldn't run back down Swanston Street as it was too well lit, and I didn't know if any of his half-baked mates would be there waiting for me. I reached the outer wall of the university, trying to figure out where to go to next. I saw a driveway leading into the college grounds, on the bend, only fifty yards away.

So could he!

I got there only ten yards in front of the Pom. He was swearing at me from behind, but I was concentrating on getting through the almost total darkness cast by a large canopy of trees lining each side of the drive. Up ahead there was a light on the side of a building to the right that helped get my bearings and make it through this black hole.

I knew he was getting close when I could see the loose gravel he kicked up fly in front of me. This mad bugger was too big to stop and take on. He probably beats up young blokes like me every other day of the week.

As the drive came to an end, it opened onto a roundabout which was well lit by the light from the building. I hit the roundabout and turned sharply to the right before my feet slipped out from under me, my boots having lost their tread years ago.

A moment later the Pom laid his boots into me, kicking me once in the back of my right leg and then straight for my head. I curled up like a baby, covering my face with my arms, uselessly trying to protect myself. He kept kicking until he opened up a cut under my chin; blood flowing freely.

It felt like there was metal cutting into me. I desperately had to do something to stop him. He screamed like a madman that he was 'gonna friggin kill me'.

I grabbed one of his legs, just to get a reprieve from his boots. Suddenly the Pom was violently jerked backwards by a force powerful enough to lift him off his feet. His dungaree-clad assailant, who had appeared out of nowhere, released the flailing body of the Englishman in mid-air, leaving him to fall helplessly, the back of his head hitting the ground hard, then the rest of his large body followed, flattening out under its weight.

Thank God! But who was this bloke?

I caught a glimpse of the assailant's face beneath a peaked cap as he looked around to see if anyone was witnessing this little tiff, before he leant down to hit the dog hard, five or six times to the face; blood poured from the Pom's mouth.

"You men ... you men there," a man's voice cried out, "that's enough ... that's more than enough!"

Squinting through a wall of light, I could make out the silhouette of a man in a second floor window. Behind him other figures were approaching the glass.

"Are you animals? ... Well are you?" shouted the man in the window, obviously missing the matinée show. "Can't you see this man is unconscious?" His cultured voice rose to a high pitch, "He needs medical attention." He paused for a moment, turning to say something to the figures milling around him.

Then I heard: "You owe me, Sunshine."

I looked back down on hearing this voice but my very welcome guest had gone, taking the opportunity to disappear like I should have.

The man in the window continued in a high pitched voice. "Don't you go anywhere, I'm coming down."

There was no doubt this bloke was a professor by the way he spoke, but I had no intention of waiting around with him until the coppers came to pick me up. The ones around here have a bad habit of giving everyone they round up a good belting, just for the fun of it.

I had to move quickly, as the professor wouldn't take long to get downstairs. Though, what worried me now was my Pommy mate. He had begun to cough up blood, and hadn't moved his arms or legs since he was hit more times than necessary by my rescuer. I'm sure a tough bugger like him could take a punch, but rightly or wrongly, I was getting out of here.

The first thing I had to do was get out of the light, so I ran directly under a blanket of shadow covering the building that housed the professor and his friends. Looking upwards I could make out several heads peering over the second floor ledge searching for me as I stayed tight against the wall below. They gave up shortly afterwards unable to make anything out in the pitch blackness.

I moved quickly in the direction of where I thought Swanston Street might be, sneaking over to an even larger building, in line with the first, before stopping in the shadows of a buttress, two hundred yards further on. From the buttress, I could see people moving as shadows in the vicinity of the roundabout, a torch light flashing occasionally in my direction.

Why did I hit that bloody Irishman? Now, the Pom's in real trouble.

My right thigh muscle was cramping now at the spot

where I had been kicked, and felt as tight as a drum. I couldn't raise a slow jog, even if the whole damn Magenta Push were on my tail.

There was a building opposite my hideaway, much smaller than any of the college buildings I had seen so far. It was surrounded by a thick, shoulder-high hedge and a good covering of shrubs. It would offer more protection than the buttress, and the driveway was probably on the other side of it.

I'm sure the police wouldn't be too far away, either. So, my plan was simple — as soon as the coppers arrive, shoot through.

Whoever had the torch must have decided to move their search to another section of the grounds, as all of a sudden darkness came over my immediate surrounds. I took the opportunity to drag myself towards the smaller building, bending down low behind a row of shrubs. Through the foliage, I could make out a group of four or five people looking out from the roundabout and then inwards again, before pointing in all directions. No-one was bending down, so perhaps the Pom had been taken to an infirmary inside the college building.

I was starting to get the lie of the land from my new position; this building was a good distance from the main college buildings, which to my mind made it a good spot to skip out of this trap. One at a time, the group at the roundabout began to disperse. One person headed my way, towards the smaller building which was only ten yards to the left of me. Of course someone lived there. I took a peek over the top of the shrubs to get a better look. It was only when the person stepped clear of a shadow that I realised it was a woman. She was pulling a dressing gown tight around her, probably warding off the sudden chill that had crept in.

I was surprised that a woman would be walking on her own, considering what had just happened; after all dangerous 'animals' were in the grounds. Before she reached the building, she stopped and then turned around slowly to look towards the roundabout. She turned back again, staring in my direction. This seemed to go on for minutes, before she walked to within a couple of yards of me.

"You're one of the young men in the fight, aren't you?" the woman asked.

I didn't say a word and crouched lower behind the shrubs, not wanting to accept the mess I was in, wishing this woman would just go away.

"I saw most of the fight, you know. Your mate didn't have to hit that man when he was down." The woman continued in a proper voice, "It was uncalled for ... he was unconscious."

I looked up through the shrubs again as she had turned back towards the roundabout. I wanted to call out to her, but I couldn't make myself. I was totally deflated by my own stupidity. I expected her to scream out for help any second.

"You're lucky your opponent got up before. He wiped his face with a wet towel, trying to stop the bleeding. He kept repeating that he was going to get you — and your friend. He was adamant about that. The professor said he should wait for an ambulance and the police to arrive, but he wouldn't have anything to do with that. Nothing we said would stop him from leaving."

I was relieved to hear that he was gone, but I didn't need a lecture. It wasn't her head that was getting kicked in.

"When the police arrive they will put in a concerted effort to find you both," the woman said without emotion. "What do you think about that?" She stopped for a second, waiting for me to respond before continuing, "I've seen the Englishman before on Lygon Street. I know he's a thug. So you must have done something pretty stupid for him to chase you this far?"

I stayed silent.

"Look, you're probably a good kid and feeling bad about what's happened. I can show you a path that will take you out of the grounds, it's just nearby ..."

The woman hesitated. "But, I think it would be better if you cleaned yourself up first and then moved on. You won't attract as much attention on your way home."

I should say something to her. I need to stop acting like a child.

"You need to make a choice," she said firmly before turning around to walk to the smaller building, going inside and shutting the door behind her.

My Aunty May thinks she can read people. I wasn't too sure about that. She's always telling me to be wary of people, especially overly friendly ones. "They're probably trying to fleece you out of everything you've got." She should know, she'd had a few smarmy types fleece her before. I can't be like Aunty May.

I snuck over to the building and knocked quietly on the door. There was no other sound except the door slowly opening. A middle-aged woman stepped into the frame of the doorway, one hand on her hip the other holding her well-worn dressing gown tight. Her features were pale, almost non-existent outside of her dark-brown eyes securely fixed on me; fine hair floated across her forehead in the gentle breeze. She looked me up and down as if I was something that the cat had just left on the mat, making me wait on the porch so that anyone, including the people still looking for me, could see the poor unfortunate that was in need of her help.

"I'm not who you think I am," I said close to tears. "I only made one mistake tonight."

"You are a young man, too small to take on the Englishman," the woman stated, opening the door fully. "In one way you did well."

She stepped back for me to walk into her lounge room.

A blanket thrown over an old leather couch was the only seating in the room, a small bookshelf and a low table, the only other furniture. She walked down an unlit passage without saying a word. I followed cautiously and then joined her in a room with a table and chairs in the middle. I presumed it was the kitchen, but with only a small amount of reflected light from the lounge, it was difficult to tell.

She told me to sit down, while she fumbled about in a drawer, finally lighting a candle, before sitting next to me at the table.

"Do you work at Gennons?" she asked. "You definitely have a sheep smell about you?"

Strewth! Does everyone know what I do for a quid?

"No, I work at a fellmongers in North Melbourne. They're only small."

"You don't have to tell me the name of the company if you don't want." Her tone softened.

"They're called Cooks," I replied, starting to feel a little more at ease with this woman. "We push through a lot of skins each week."

"Put your head back," the woman said suddenly. "You have something hanging from under your chin."

I felt immediately under my chin, surprised to find a good-sized piece of skin hanging free, although I could barely feel it. Before I could say no, the woman had pulled a pair of scissors out from a drawer and told me to hold still. I felt only the slightest sting as she cut away the offending skin and my eyes started to water.

"Sorry, I should have said something outside," I mumbled to myself. "I just froze. My name is Sebastian. I live with my aunt in Carlton. The rest of the family are in the country."

"Your aunt will be worried then."

I could make out her face now, as the candlelight flickered over it. She had quite a pretty face for an older woman. I watched her loose, mousey hair fly in all directions as she moved, strands floating in front of her face as she pulled out a towel from a nearby cupboard and handed it to me.

"Head out the back, Sebastian. You can wash yourself in the gully trap."

I didn't like the idea of going outside yet and it must have shown on my face.

"Don't worry, you won't be seen from the grounds unless you're silly enough to stand on top of the trap. Give me your shirt. I'll sponge some of the blood out of it. I'm sure it gets messy most days at work, but not as much as this."

I had hesitated for a second before the woman jumped in.

"I have three younger brothers," she snapped, holding out her hand.

I undid my braces, pulling the shirt over my head in a slow painful movement. She snatched my shirt, before leading me out a door at the far end of the kitchen. Outside, she pointed me in the direction of the gully trap, and gently closed the screen door behind her as she went back inside. I started cleaning the sticky layer of blood and muck from my face, neck and arms, the cold water bringing me back to the here and now, and also soothing a well and truly bruised and battered body.

When I returned to the kitchen, the woman was sitting in front of a stove. She had made a pot of tea, placed a cup and saucer in front of the chair where I had been seated, and was now slicing into a small chocolate cake. She told me that if I wanted to eat, I had to sit down first.

I wanted to ask her name, but I thought it might be wiser not to. After all, she was hiding someone in the grounds that staff from her own college were looking for. If I didn't know her name, how could I possibly dob her in.

She had made me so comfortable that I momentarily forgot that the police, and perhaps some of the boys from the Magenta Push may still be outside looking for me.

I hoed into the tea and cake, not believing food could taste so good.

"I thought you might be famished," the woman said kindly as she sat down next to me.

"You're not the first person to come into the college grounds in a spot of trouble. The Depression has been going on for quite a while now," she explained, looking at me with tiredness in her eyes. "A lot of people camp rough in Princes Park. Sometimes their disputes spill over onto our campus."

"That's not me, and the bloke that hit the Pom is no mate of mine," I jumped in, defensively. "He's probably an 'obo from Princes Park, but I'm bloody glad he came along when he did. I'm just a fellmonger, which is nothing, but I didn't come down from the country to be a burden on anyone, and I won't be."

I shivered, before remembering I didn't have my shirt on. It was hanging over the metal handle of the oven. The woman felt the collar before handing it to me, without saying a word.

It was hard to tell what this woman was thinking, her face didn't give away a thing, and that included whether she believed a word I was saying.

Our little tea party came to an abrupt end with the sound of knocking on the front door.

"Get out to the trap," she said sharply, pointing me towards the rear door of the kitchen, and then quickly snuffed out the candle.

As I sat on the wet gully trap, I suddenly felt waves of exhaustion come over me, relieved at being well sheltered from prying eyes; on my left, a solid wooden screen blocked the main college buildings, two yards in front of me a thick hedge. But, the longer I stayed outside, the less concerned I became if I was sprung or not. It was the middle of the night and I was freezing.

I was also busting for a wee, right here, right now. So, I snuck around the hedge and found a tree large enough for me to hide behind, while praying that the woman didn't come outside, not quite yet.

As luck would have it the woman stuck her head out the screen door whispering, "Sebastian, you'd better go now, the police will be back in a half an hour to do a full sweep of the grounds. Go right away. Take the path on the left, don't mind if it becomes overgrown, just keep going."

Before I could say anything to this woman who had done so much to help an injured stray, she was gone, closing the door quietly behind her, leaving me in the stony silence of the college grounds.

I wanted to go home badly and I knew my aunt would be beyond herself with worry that I didn't turn up for her special dinner, but the route home was too close to Magenta Lane. To stay as far away from its notorious Push was the most important thing I could do tonight. I would make my way back to Cooks and then wait for my workmates to turn up in the morning. I could suffer any consequences, later.

Fortunately, the only soul on the streets of Parkville at the moment was the milko doing his rounds. I kept my head down as I waved to him while I crossed over Royal Parade, before heading down Gatehouse, over Flemington Road and then worked my way through the back streets of North Melbourne until I reached the industrial area.

Once I reached Cooks, I collapsed against a light pole in front of the factory, not even aware when I fell asleep.

*

"Carmichael!"

I woke with a jolt and the sight of my foreman sneering down at me.

"Do you know the state your aunt is in?"

"What ...?" I managed to mumble "What's happened?" I couldn't focus or think clearly. I tried to stand, but my right leg didn't want to do what I told it.

"Are you drunk?" the foreman yelled. "Is this the gratitude you give your aunt?"

"I'm not drunk. I haven't had anything to drink," I said finally managing to stand myself up.

"I couldn't make it home last night, that's all. I had to come back here to sleep." I wished more than anything that this mean bastard hadn't taken a room at my aunt's boarding house. He thinks he owns the bloody place.

"Bullshit!" the foreman snarled "You'll pay a pretty penny when you get home tonight ... you little shit," he said throwing me a brown paper bag, which I hoped to hell had sandwiches in it.

"Your aunt thinks way too much of you, Carmichael," the foreman scoffed, before pushing open the corrugated iron factory gate to let the workers in.

I followed grudgingly, shoving my right hand deep into my pocket, surprised to find at the bottom, an unusual object; too large and light to be a penny. I pulled it out quickly, knowing it wasn't mine. On closer examination, it turned out to be a large brown button, on the outer side it read 'Food for Spain'.

2

Aunty May

From somewhere deep inside the Leidgen Drum, an annoying scraping sound was repeating every five seconds, much like fingernails running down a blackboard. I moved closer to the ugly beast of a machine, and then further away from it, trying to locate without any luck the source of this relentless noise. It didn't seem to bother the other blokes in the de-woolling shop though.

The shop seemed completely different to me today, maybe it was the night I'd just had. I wasn't sure. But this factory with rotting sheepskins lying everywhere and no fresh air to breathe, seemed more like a stinking prison than the wonderful opportunity I thought it might have been six months ago. At least in prison, your wages aren't docked if your 'task' isn't met.

Instead of the Leidgen Drum, I should have been thinking about which quiet back streets to take to avoid running into the probably livid Magenta Push on my way back home — and then everywhere else for the rest of my perhaps short life. Or, how many strips my Aunty May could possibly tear off her very tired nephew before he could make it upstairs and crawl into bed, in the cramped little room at the back of her doss house tonight.

More than anything it was the young man who took down the Pom in the college, who I couldn't figure out. Who was he and why had he helped me at all, or was he just another thug from another push evening up an old score? Also, why would a woman go against the police and her own college to hide a stranger and then help them escape? I don't think I would have done the same thing in their place. I looked at the button again to see if it offered a clue, but the more I tried to make sense out of it and last night, the more confusing it all became.

"Hello, Sebastian. How are you?" the foreman asked, standing to the left of me with a stupid grin on his face. "Enjoying the view? Is there anything I can get for you? A chair, perhaps."

I knew I would be in for some sort of treatment today; better to get it over and done with.

"No, I think I'm fine. Thanks, just the same," I said knowing he would have put some serious thought into humiliating me after witnessing my pitiful appearance this morning.

The foreman had brought out a chair from his office and a small worktable covered in a white tarpaulin from the skin-dressing room. He directed the table and chair to be placed in front of me and then, just like a waiter, the foreman held back the chair for me to sit down.

With this sort of thing, it's best to play along with their childish games; it annoys them if you don't.

One of the old boys brought out a dirty vase with a frizzled Scotch-thistle stuck inside, placing it on the table in front of me, before bowing as he moved to the side.

The foreman really has put a lot of thought into this.

The leading-hand came out of the dressing room with a small white towel over his left arm, a dusty wine bottle in his grubby right hand. His idiot off-sider Lenny followed close behind, carrying a tray with God-knows-what hidden under an old towel.

"Would you like to taste it first, Sebastian?" asked the leading-hand, ready to burst.

"No, I'm sure it will be fine, just the way it is," I replied, closing my eyes in anticipation.

I waited for about twenty seconds and then another twenty seconds.

What the hell were they up to?

I opened my left eye to take a quick peek.

Thwack!

They all let loose with handfuls of wet sheep dags, hitting me squarely on my screwed up face, some direct-ed at my defenseless crutch, laughter breaking out all over the factory floor.

"Go on, Sebastian. Go home," shouted the foreman. "You're making the blowies look good."

The foreman was almost wetting himself with laughter,

along with the rest of the crew, as he lifted me up and shoved me gently towards the exit door. Lenny threw me the old towel from the tray, so I could give myself a rough clean down before I left, maybe feeling sorry for a young lad who had to walk home with little bits of dirty wool stuck all over him.

*

I decided to see if last night's plan to take the northern route back home really was a good way to whip around the Magenta Push and reach the relative safety of Aunty May's. I went back through Parkville, over Royal Parade and then skirted the College Crescent next to the Melbourne University, almost tempted to go back into the grounds again, so I could say thanks to the woman who had helped me.

Most likely, she would be working and the last person she would want to see, or anyone else involved for that matter, is the young scrapper who kept them up half the night, coming back in the middle of the next day, looking like no-one owned him. When fellmongers send you on your way, you must be in a bad state. So, perhaps the less people see of me, the better.

Against my better judgment, I began to walk down a section of Lygon Street I had only ventured to a couple of times since I made the big move down to the city, surprised to see how many people were out and about at this time of day.

For some reason, I thought most people had to work in similarly horrible jobs as me during the day, but after watching harassed mothers dragging their bratty kids along behind them, while lugging brown paper packets in cane baskets and manoeuvering around mobs of men in tatty clothes, hanging about on street corners, factory work seemed a smidge less terrible.

During school holidays years ago, my sister Lettie and I were often sent up this way by our Aunty May, on a mission to the grocer, to get the flour or sugar she seemed to run out of regularly in the kitchen. Lettie and I eventually worked out that it was a pretty good ruse to get us out of the house, when we were beginning to get under her feet. We definitely got the better end of the deal, as she often gave us a penny each to buy whatever we wanted, which was usually a huge bag of lollies or a double cone ice-cream.

The old Jewish grocer loved to play tricks on the kids who regularly came into his store. When Lettie and I dropped in an order, he would weigh the sugar or flour, wrap it up and hand me the packet, pretending to forget about the ice-creams or lollies we had ordered. I would go to leave, carefully watching the look on Lettie's face as she began to panic, thinking that the grocer had forgotten our treats. At the point when her bottom lip started to quiver, the grocer would call out, "Did anyone order ice-creams?"

Lettie's arm would go up in a flash. She fell for that for years.

As I approached the old grocer's store, a small army of workmen were pulling the shop apart. I looked through the dust and rubble into the shell, but couldn't see the old fella anywhere. He must have moved on.

After passing the Albion Hotel, I realised was getting too close to Magenta Lane for my liking, thinking it wiser to cut across to Drummond Street at Faraday, to avoid the Magenta Push's stomping ground.

I turned into Drummond, glad to see only a couple of people on the street. One was a shabbily dressed man in a long black crumpled coat who must have been boiling under all his garb, while the other was a young boy. They were both a long way ahead, walking in the same direction as me.

The man looked like a lot of other blokes wandering the streets, down on their luck, all their belongings in a hessian bag slung over their shoulder. The young boy in shorts and a grubby singlet seemed happy enough, a few steps behind, poking his stick at rubbish in the gutter.

I was more than a little intrigued when the man suddenly motioned for the boy to follow him quickly into a laneway.

I poked my head around a rosebush to look down the

lane, and there they were, standing under the swaying branches of a weeping willow tree. As the unkempt man leant his hessian bag and himself up against a fence in the shade of the tree, he appeared nothing more than any other unemployed man travelling with his young son, only wanting a quiet spot to rest out of the sun until the cool of the evening.

I was about to move on, when the man walked over to the paling fence opposite and bent down low in front of it. The next second the young boy ran at him like a miniature acrobat and in one leap and a bound cleared the fence, vanishing into someone's backyard.

Sneaky buggers!

The next second, a couple of apples flew over the fence into a hessian bag held wide open by the man, who was moving it to suit the trajectory of his prize. Zucchinis, tomatoes and a cabbage, or was that a lettuce, arcing over the fence. I suppose if you're starving hungry, you have to get creative.

The young boy was back over the fence in a flash, using the rails on the yard-side to get a leg up and a quick getaway. In one minute they had procured enough food for a few days' meals and then they were gone. I didn't even see which way they went at the far end of the lane.

Bravo, tiny circus troupe!

I was not expecting to see such an ingenious perfor-mance on a quiet workday afternoon. I kept looking down the lane just in case someone leapt over the fence in pursuit of them. After a minute, a woman wearing a red scarf poked her head cautiously over the fence. She looked left and then right, before spitting over the fence, while grumbling something in a foreign tongue. She lowered herself slowly back into the yard, probably needing to take an inventory of what was left of her veggie patch.

Now, I knew why the good people of Carlton were giving every transient the 'evil eye'.

After a hundred yards, I caught the very welcome sight of the cream walls of Aunty May's boarding house. As soon as I reached the backyard I squatted down to drink big gulps of cool water straight from the garden tap. Out of the corner of my eye I caught sight of someone standing to my left with a strong scent of lavender on them.

Aunty May!

"Sebastian?" asked Aunty May, in a haughty voice. "Are we having the honour of your company tonight, or will you be tomcatting again this evening?" She had nicely extracted every ounce of sarcasm from each word.

She leant down in her loose floral summer dress to look closely at me. I jumped back with a start.

"Well, if you're a tomcat, you're not a very good one," Aunty May quipped. "Look at yourself. Your father fancied himself as a pugilist, but he wasn't any good either. Didn't stop him though ... too stubborn. You're a lot like your father in many respects, Sebastian."

Give me strength!

I made a move towards the stairs that led up to my digs, embarrassed now by my stench. I needed to spend the whole evening in the washroom scrubbing myself until it hurts, not wanting to think about the day-and-a-half of the working week I still had left.

"Well, go on then, get going, but I want you back downstairs quick smart," Aunty May ordered "I have something to tell you that I wanted to tell you last night."

I hesitated for a second, trying to think what the hurry up could be about.

"Well! ... Haven't you kept me waiting long enough?"

*

On returning to the kitchen, Aunty May offered me a milk arrowroot biscuit from her fancy embossed tin, before sitting down next to me at our long, lace-covered communal table.

"Sebastian, you know how difficult things have been in the hostellerie industry," Aunty May stated, staring at me strangely with her head leant to one side.

Hostellerie! Why does she have to use fancy words?

I woofed down the biscuit and then started to chew on my nails.

"Don't do that Sebastian, it's so common," Aunty May huffed as she straightened in her chair.

"Unfortunately, my tenants think that beer, tobacco and betting are the be all and end all. Well, there's a rude awakening coming for them. We are just keeping our heads above water at the moment, Sebastian. Lord knows how much worse things would be if Barry wasn't here to help us. He's such a wonderful man you know, a godsend really. I can't tell you how much he does around here."

Why is she telling me this? And how could she ever think that slippery snake, my foreman, could in any way resemble a wonderful godsend? I wonder what scam he's working on her.

"Aunty, you said you had some news..." I inquired trying to get her focus off Barry.

"Oh, yes I do. I received a letter from your parents a couple of days ago and I think you will like some of it. I was going to tell you all about it over a fine dinner last night, but as it happens, Barry enjoyed your lambs fry," Aunty May stopped suddenly to grab my arm and blurted out.

"Leticia's coming to Melbourne. She's arriving by train on Tuesday."

"Lettie coming to Melbourne?" I paused, stunned for a second.

"And there's a possibility it may be permanent," Aunty May added cautiously.

"Wow! What great news," I continued, trying to hold down my excitement.

I stood up and walked around the kitchen, suddenly wide awake after beginning to flag.

"Gosh, I can't tell you how good it will be to have Lettie around," I added, almost to myself.

Then I sat down as quickly as I got up, realising there might be more to this news than I first thought.

"I hope nothing has happened back home to make Lettie have to come down so suddenly."

"According to your parents," Aunt May said reading from the letter, "they want Leticia to 'broaden her horizons' by trying to find a permanent position in the city. They don't see many prospects for her in the country."

Aunty May put the letter down and continued with her arms crossed.

"Well, in my opinion, if she took some of my advice regarding her dress she might have a better chance of finding suitable employment, or even a well-connected suitor."

"Lettie's only eighteen, Aunty. She has plenty of time to find her place in the world."

"Well, I don't have plenty of time to wait for her to grow up," Aunty May jumped in. "Because, I can't afford to employ her here .... I know it's difficult for everyone at the moment, but just because your father's truck catches on fire, doesn't mean I can afford ..."

"My dad's truck caught on fire?" I shot back, surprised by her off-handedness. "When?"

"He didn't say when, Sebastian, I think he's embarrassed by the whole affair. He's not a farmer's backside you know, or a good business man for that matter. Sometimes, I think it would be better if your older brother Vernon took over. It seems to come naturally to him. I would love it if that beautiful boy came down to visit more often. I could tell him how the Boer farmers did things differently during my visit to the Cape Colony. They know how to make the most out of neglected country," Aunty May's eyes starting to wander around the room.

Here we go ...

I wanted to find out what happened with Dad's truck, knowing without the cash it brings in, it could cause a lot of hardship to the family. But, I thought in this case, it might be better to wait until Tuesday, so I could get the news first-hand from Lettie.

"Was there any mention of Robbie in the letter, Aunty?" I asked, hoping if there was, it was good. The last I heard, Robbie was refusing to help out around the farm and only wanted to read in his room, which was upsetting the rest of the family no end.

"Robert?" Aunty May paused for a second as if she wasn't sure who I was talking about.

"No, no mention of Robert. But, that boy does need to get his head out of the clouds. He can't run away from reality forever. A life in the military would turn him around; turn him into a man. It would have been good for your father too, but he decided to stay at home with the women during the Great War. Your Uncle Will had to pay the ultimate price in France. He was such a huge loss to the family you know. Although, I never agreed with the white feathers your father received, I do understand that not everyone has the fight in them."

I could bloody throttle her. If she ever pulled her head out of her arse, she would remember that staying behind on the farm was the hardest decision my dad ever had to make. He was ordered to stay at home for the duration because my grandfather was a good forty years older than him and struggling to cope. A letter came directly from the Minister of Defence, stating that the provision of goods, like wool and oats, was like having a hundred men in the field.

Mum said that when they received the news of Will being killed in action, Dad was close to ending up in the asylum. She said the happy-go-lucky spirit he once had, never returned.

Aunty May knew all this.

I needed to change the subject quickly, before I said something I couldn't take back.

"Have you heard of anyone hiring at the moment, Aunty?" I asked, trying to appear cheerful. "Lettie is such a good cook."

"Well, I'm glad you asked because I did come across an advertisement recently calling for junior sales assistants in the beauty section of Myer. If Leticia showed a little more interest in her personal grooming, she might stand a chance of getting put on the books. But, I fear that the cafeteria is probably her best chance," Aunty May said, without batting an eyelid.

"I blame your mother for being too soft. She needed to be firmer with Leticia and Robert's upbringing, instead of raising money for drifters and no-hopers. I will make it my duty to turn Leticia into a lady, when she gets down here."

That was it! She was going to cop it now.

"Aunty May. My mum is the most ..." I was forced to stop mid-sentence, by the appearance of the foreman just returning from work at the screen door. A smile appeared on his face at seeing Aunty May, before quickly disappearing when he noticed I was in the kitchen as well.

Please tell me there's nothing going on between them.

I turned my head to look at the dry food containers.

"Hello, Barry. Did you have a nice day?" asked Aunty May in a sickly sweet tone.

"Yes, thanks May. We had a bit of fun today, but there we will be no room for shenanigans, tomorrow."

"Barry, you are such a gentleman for letting Sebastian finish early today. It gave us the opportunity to have a good natter and I think you will find an improved performance from him in the morning."

"I appreciate that May, but everyone at Cooks looks out for Sebastian, we wouldn't let anything bad happen to him there. You don't have to worry about him at all," lied the foreman giving me a wink and Aunty May a wave as he headed off to his room.

I'd heard enough bull for the rest of my days, so I got up and headed for the screen door, turning to look at Aunty May as I opened it.

"I will find a job for Leticia, Aunty, so you don't have to worry about her becoming a liability. See ya for tea."

I was out the screen door before Aunty May could close her mouth to open it again, letting the slam of the door become the final word on the matter.

Lettie's as smart as a whip and the hardest worker, I assured myself, before I made my way up the back steps and across to my room. Surely, between the two of us, we could find her some kind of work.

3

Aid for Spain

I could barely wait for the foreman to ring the knock-off bell at midday, so I could slam my dad's old Gladstone bag shut and get the hell out of this rotten place.

The factory had been like an oven all week and even the old-timers were dragging their sorry faces around like they'd never been through a hot spell before.

"Lucky it's Saturday," the leading hand's off-sider, Lenny, yelled out several times in the morning, driving everyone up the wall with his endless chatter.

I don't know what happened to him, no-one does, but just when you think he hasn't got a clue, he comes up with some real cracking ideas. He's probably the best mate I have here.

At smoko I made the mistake of telling Lenny that instead of going back to my digs after work, which would be like a furnace until the cool change came in later in the evening, I was going to look for a place somewhere outside the city that might be interesting to take my sister to, after she arrives on Tuesday.

"Leave it up to me, young fella," Lenny bragged while

wiping his forehead with a grotty oil-covered handkerchief. "Before the foreman rings the bell. I'll think of somewhere really grand for you to take your sister."

Gees! Anything could happen here. Lenny's mind doesn't work like other people, which wasn't necessarily a bad thing, but I wouldn't even hazard a guess where he'd want to send us.

The heat and never wanting to see the foreman again, weren't the only reasons I didn't want to head back to my tiny room after work. I had been thinking about what Aunty May had told me was in the letter from my folks. They wanted Lettie to 'broaden her horizons' down here, which was great but after six months in the city my horizons were still as flat as the Wimmera plains.

I needed a future that didn't involve sheepskins.

Six months ago, I was given the best lesson in how to prepare for the future. Make your own plans before someone else does it for you. My new life arrived one afternoon while I was working at home on the farm, in the form of a telegram from Aunty May.

'SEND SEB NOW STOP WORK STOP.'

That's all it took for me to be given an encouraging pat on the back from my family and a shove onto the next train heading towards the big smoke, without a clue as to what I'd be doing, who I'd be doing it for, or whether I'd ever make a zack out of it or not.

Aunty May had been talking to my foreman after work

one evening, when he mentioned that he had to sack an old timer called Blacky. Apparently, he'd been knocking off some of the blokes' money from their kits in the change room while pretending to go to the toilet. The foreman and the leading hand forced him to own up by threatening to send him for a spin in the Leidgen Drum if he didn't.

I would have owned up too!

Aunty May talked her new boarder and erstwhile friend Barry into leaving the position open for a few days until I made it down. She said I would work the first two days for free, as a trial. My foreman likes cheap labour.

I was brought back from my thoughts by Lenny, true to his word, turning up a minute before the knock-off bell.

"I know just the place for you, young Seb," yapped Lenny like an excited pup.

"Emerald Hill in South Melbourne is where you should take your sister. She'll love it. What they have there is what women want. Do you know what that is, Master Seb?"

"No, I don't know, Len," I replied, wondering how he could possibly know so much about women.

"Shopping, Seb. Not the snooty shopping like you see in Collins Street, where everything costs a year's wages. No, they want shops where they can buy the raw materials to make the fancy stuff for themselves. Drapers, haberdashers and grocers, that's the type of shopping women want. They like beautiful houses and gardens, too," Lenny exclaimed.

"I have also heard of gatherings that happen there from time to time, where assorted cranks get up on an old crate, sprouting their plans to save the world. I'm told it's the funniest thing you'll ever see in your life. And, you know what? It won't cost you a penny. What do you reckon of that, young Seb?"

"I like it, Lenny," I replied genuinely, "I really do." I had heard the South Melbourne area was a nice place to go to. Though, I'm not sure I would mention the fact that Lenny and I had similar ideas.

"Righto, Lenny. I'm off then," I shouted when the foreman finally rang the knock-off bell.

I knew Lenny was planning on being my guide for the day, and I should ask him, but I couldn't do it.

"Thanks for givin' me the good oil, Lenny. See ya Monday mornin'."

I felt bad when I turned around to see Lenny still waving at me as he closed the factory gate, but some people you need to have a break from.

*

I headed south along King Street, a hot northerly wind at my back, past Flagstaff Gardens which was packed with every man and his dog searching for relief from the oppressive heat. Families had laid out picnic rugs under shady trees, despite the best efforts of their kids and a gusting wind to up-end them. Groups of office workers shared patches of shade. Ties were loosened on their white Pelaco shirts, as they celebrated the end of the working week by knocking down well-earned but probably warm bottles of beer.

People became scarcer the further I went down King Street on my way towards Emerald Hill with the notable exception of every pub along the route, where large groups of men were crowded shoulder to shoulder at the bar, licensees doing a ripper trade on such a stinker of a day.

Before I moved down to the city my folks warned me to give the pubs a big miss. In a couple of months I would turn twenty-one, old enough to drink at a bar. I didn't need too much convincing to refrain from developing the habit, after seeing the results of a six o'clock swill. It was a real eye-opener to watch blokes fighting like animals to get to the bar as the 'last-drinks' bell rang, stepping over drunks passed out on the floor in a filthy pool of beer, and other vile liquids, so they could order another five or six beers.

I enjoy a beer as much as the next, when I can get my hands on one, but the sight of paralytic men pouring out of pubs at six o'clock had put me off ever wanting to join them.

Back on the farm when we were young tackers, Dad sometimes used to let us have a sip out of his glass of beer in the evening. It didn't happen very often, but when he let us, we thought he was the greatest dad ever. A couple of years later, Lettie and I snuck a bottle of his beer from the safe, left it to cool in the river overnight, and then went back the next day to knock it down. Thinking back now, he must have known it was us.

I still think it's funny that Lettie is the only girl I know who likes the taste of beer.

One of the favourite things that Lettie liked to do when we came down to the city as kids was to go up front with Aunty May on the dummy of the cable tram. To fly past the huge crowds and tall buildings in the city, and then to hang on for dear life around the bends was a dream for us country kids.

On one trip, when the grip-man released the cable too early, the tram was left stranded half-way around the bend at Parliament House. All the passengers had to get out and push the tram into Bourke Street, but few of them thought it was as funny as Lettie and I did.

Going for a ride on a cable tram, will be the first thing Lettie will want to do on Tuesday night.

I felt almost overwhelmed by the stifling heat as I crossed over Flinders Street, happy to see the Yarra River only a short distance ahead. I found myself a shady spot on the dock of the ship turning basin, hidden away between the Spencer Street Bridge and an old wreck of a barge, hoping that one of the quietest parts of the city could provide me with the perfect refuge to ponder my biggest dilemma. How could I possibly help Lettie find work down here?

Lettie walked away from a part-time job in a drapers back home; she may regret that. Down here she would have to become a real grafter, jumping on every opportunity that popped its head up, if she wanted to get to the front of the long queues beside every 'positions vacant' sign.

As the wind slowly changed direction, it was too hot to think about work or anything else, except hopping into the round of sandwiches I had made in the morning, and drinking some of the lukewarm water that I thankfully remembered to put in a spare Cottee's bottle before I left the factory. As I relaxed into my own private picnic, my thoughts drifted back to my family in the country, wondering what turmoil the letter from my folks was hiding.

A couple of cars and motorbikes crossing over the bridge were the only things moving at any pace at the moment. If they had any sense, they would either head east towards the cool of the Dandenong hills or south towards a sandy beach on the bay.

*

After lunch, I reluctantly left my shady spot by the river walking up onto Spencer Street Bridge which was baking under the blazing afternoon sun. From the middle of the bridge, I couldn't miss the signs of the cool change to come. A long, dark line of cloud spread across the horizon to the west, pushing heavy humid air in front of it. I couldn't wait for it to get here.

I stopped briefly in the shadow of a huge storage facility; the words 'Tea House' were blazoned in large lettering across the top storey of the imposing building.

It made me think about what my friend Arty told me a few days before I moved down to Melbourne, in a poor effort to make me change my mind. "You know the buildings in the city block out the sun, Seb. That's why city folk always look so pale and sickly."

Arty really doesn't know what he's talking about, he's only been to Melbourne once.

I stayed in the shadows of as many buildings as I could while heading up the slope towards the main shopping strip of Clarendon Street.

I reached the first canopy of the shopping strip, a little reluctant to wade into the tangled mass of shoppers, who milled in front of shop windows and jammed up doors, as far as the eye could see. After weaving my way through the crowd to one display, it became clear what the fuss was all about.

Bargains!

Almost every shop had a 'Sale' sign in the window and every other shop a 'Prices Reduced' sign. Several had spruikers out front making outrageous claims about the quality of their goods. One shop, which was doing rather well, was a kitchenware store that had a large array of shiny new pots and pans, at 'unbelievable' prices. Lettie won't go past this shop I could guarantee it.

I couldn't believe so many people, with so little money, could hand over so much of it. Lenny had hit the nail on the head when he said this was the place for people that loved shopping.

There was a longish queue in front of a grocery store called Carruthers. On the outside, it looked like any other grocers, but after looking past the crowd to the inside, things appeared decidedly different.

In the middle of each aisle, large tins of virtually every foodstuff known to man were stacked precariously high, assistants in pristine white uniforms fussing over each shopper's smallest request. Personally, I prefer not to be bothered when I shop, which is a rarity in itself, but the customers here didn't seem to mind the pushy approach because they were buying, and buying a lot. After ten minutes, an elderly male assistant pulled me aside from the crush, telling me I ought to buy something fairly soon or I could get out, and that he would be watching me the whole time I stayed in there. Their friendliness was for paying customers only.

As a 'Reduced by Half' sign was placed on a large stack of tins nearby, I was shoved aside by almost rabid shoppers, trying in a mad rush to get their hands on the huge cans of whole beetroots, the stack reduced to half within seconds. This shop has found a way of beating our rotten economy by selling food cheap enough to fill hungry stomachs.

There were a few funny smells coming from the sweaty customers pushing me back and forth, so I thought I would give the old bugger still watching me his wish and leave the premises, as soon as I could push and shove my way out.

A little further down from Carruthers in the busiest section so far of Clarendon Street, I noticed three young people standing behind a small trestle table, perched close to the gutter. A banner behind them, tied between two verandah poles, was sign-written in large red, black and gold lettering, 'Aid for Spain'. The mention of Spain caught my attention.

Underneath the banner was a poster with 'MADRID' written in large black letters. There were other words at the bottom, too small to read from where I stood and an unusual picture in the centre. At first glance, this picture seemed to portray a swarm of mosquitoes flying past a doll with numbers on its dress. It didn't make sense to me, but due to the fact that their banner had the word 'Aid' as part of it, they were probably chasing money.

Recent newspapers had small articles about the rebellion in Spain, but they gave few details, and any news took so long to reach us from Europe, so it was difficult to tell if the war was even still going. I thought about lining up to ask one of the two young women or the young bloke about their cause, and their merchandise, but a few people were already waiting in line and I still had more to see in Emerald Hill, so I decided to keep moving. Up ahead, I noticed a greengrocer's where I might get a bite to eat for later in the afternoon.

I started to push my way back into the crowd, when a female voice called out to me from behind. "Excuse me ... young man?"

I turned around to see if the owner of this voice was calling me, which was unlikely, or someone else near me in the crowd.

"Yes you, young man."

A pretty, brunette girl, one of the helpers behind the Aid for Spain stand was calling and waving at me to come back to the trestle table.

I hesitated for a second, as a few shoppers stopped, waiting to see if I would go back to her stand or not. I did want to find out more about the poster, and how they could possibly do much good for Spain from so far away, although I was a little annoyed at being singled out in front of a street full of nosey shoppers. Surely by the look of me, this girl must know I wouldn't make much of a dent in their coffers. As I began to walk back towards the girl, a tiny smile appeared on her face.

"Thanks for coming back. I'm sorry for yelling at you like that, but I noticed you were looking at our 'Madrid' poster. I thought you might have had some questions about it."

I couldn't think of what to say for a second, pleasantly surprised at being spoken to like an adult for a change, and not merely as a worker or a kid.

"No, that's all right. I was curious about the poster."

"My name is Elaine. I'm a volunteer for the Spanish Aid Committee. We are highlighting the plight of the Spanish people, and trying to raise funds for the civilian victims of the rebel aggression. What would you like to know about the poster?" the pretty assistant asked, stepping to the side, so I had the full view.

"I was just too far back to see it clearly, that's all," I explained, now realising it wasn't a doll at all, but a young girl with dozens of warplanes passing diagonally over her head, the words on the poster calling this 'The Military practice of the Rebels'.

"What happened to this girl?" I asked, now finding the poster hard to look at.

"This girl is one of the victims of the fascist planes bombing Madrid. The rebels are being aided by German aviators in their attempt to terrorise the population of the capital. This girl was one of thirty-six children killed during an air raid. An Italian-manufactured bomb made a direct hit on her school." The young woman's eyes were beginning to well up with tears.

I felt sorry for this child as well, and all the other victims, and if I had money to burn I would give it to them, but at the moment I was nearly skint.

"I thought it was a doll." The words were already out of my mouth before I realised how cold they sounded.

The young man with messy black hair to the left of Elaine, turned from the couple he was talking to and leaned across the trestle table towards me; he had anger in his eyes, the likes of which I had seen only a few days ago during my run-in with the Pom in the grounds of the university.

"Doll!" he yelled. "That doll is someone's child, murdered by a fascist army, hell-bent on sending Spain back into the Dark Ages. Think before you speak!"

Once he had finished his tirade, he turned to face the street, away from the gaze of the people in earshot of the stand.

Elaine grabbed the young man by the arm and led him off to the side, his arms flailing about in the air, no doubt in an attempt to explain his over-reaction to my remark. I knew I had said the wrong thing, but his response didn't match my innocent slip of the tongue. I thought about waiting for him to come back, but unless I wanted to prove some silly point, the best thing I could do would be to move quietly along.

Elaine returned quickly to the stand, leaving her fellow assistant to cool off on his own. One positive outcome from our minor confrontation was that it attracted a small crowd to the trestle table, who were now keenly flicking through pamphlets, wanting to know more about the Spanish conflict.

"Sorry. I'd better go before I upset anybody else," I said, apologetically to Elaine while slowly stepping away.

"There is one way you could help if you like before you go. We have items for sale to raise money specifically for food to go to an Australian-run orphanage in Spain and to purchase an ambulance for use by an Australian team of nurses already on the frontline. We have stamps, buttons, pamphlets and lots of other merchandise, but clearly this is a donation to help innocent people in need."

"Did you say buttons?" I asked, louder than I should have, turning my head sharply to look at the young man who had yelled at me.

Was it him? Was he the same bloke that helped me at the University?

"Do you mind if I have a look at the buttons?"

"Of course you can," the young brunette said, glancing at me sideways for the briefest second.

"We also have several pamphlets that have just arrived from Spain. They contain the latest developments."

I acknowledged the young lady with a small nod, picking up a pamphlet called 'From the battlefields of Spain', which claimed progress by the Republican Government, but it was the buttons I was interested in. In a small tray there were only two types of buttons and one was the same as I had in my pocket.

Looking over at him, I was certain now that he was the same man that had helped me at the uni.

But why would he leave a button in my pocket?

"I know a lot of workers wear those buttons with pride, and hardly any of them lose their breeches," the pretty brunette joked with a cheeky grin on her face.

"Righto, you've won me," I returned, smiling back at her. "I'll get somethin'."

I bought the pamphlet and a block of stamps, just two small things to show that I wasn't as insensitive as I sounded. Elaine nodded her thanks, as I handed over my sixpence contribution to their cause.

I looked again at the still agitated young man who I was sure saved me on Wednesday night, now facing toward the stand with his hands on his hips. I owed him a lot more than a 'thanks' for what he did at the university, but after his snarling performance at the trestle table it was probably best to call things quits.

After I had moved back into the crowd along Clarendon Street, I turned around briefly to look back at the Aid for Spain stand and its young volunteers, especially my fiery wild-haired friend who had returned to the fold. He was pointing out some feature of the 'Madrid' poster to a young couple, when Elaine came up beside him and put her arm around his shoulder.

At least, they could never be accused of not believing in their cause, the young people behind the Aid for Spain stand.

4

Red Square

My sore and sorry legs felt like they needed a good stretch, well before I stepped out from the last canopy of the Clarendon Street shopping strip into a sun more forgiving as the cool change rolled in. The cramping in my black-and-blue right leg had increased considerably since the morning, and I could expect to see an unpleasant yellow tinge to it in the next couple of days.

I stopped at the greengrocer's to buy a Jonathan apple. The proprietor grumbled that it was customary to buy a bagful before I remembered to ask him if he knew of the place in South Melbourne Lenny had jabbered on about this morning, where spruikers get up on an old crate sprouting their plans to save the world. If it was half as good as Lenny claimed, it would be a real lark.

"I don't think it's around here, skinflint," the grocer grudgingly replied. "Port Melbourne sounds more like it, and I've heard the name 'Red Square' mentioned before."

Dust and leaves were swirling everywhere as black clouds gathered overhead, ushering in the cool change. I had known full well before this day was done I was going to be soaked to the skin which to my mind would be the perfect relief from the scorching heat.

I stopped for a breather on a long curving street called Ferrars, amazed by the beautiful houses in this part of South Melbourne and also the eerie lack of people on the streets. I was unsure which way to turn when I felt something rub up against my leg. I hoped it was a little luck, but it was just a grey and white moggy looking for a feed. It headed in the direction of the city, so I figured I'd do the same. I had to run into some locals soon.

I had too much time to think, as I tramped along Ferrars Street, unsettled by the vision of that poor girl in Madrid. Do the fascist pilots, safe in their planes out of range of gunfire, think about the families they're bombing, below in Madrid? If I was in their place I would find it difficult to live with.

Fifty yards down the road, I could see a couple of young lads walking my way. One swung a bat, the other bounced a ball.

Of course! The Test cricket was on today. That would explain why no-one was out and about. Both lads were wearing souvenir baggy-green caps, as they took it in turns to push each other on the shoulder while walking along as happy as Larry. When one of them was pushed near a horse trough, he took the opportunity to cup his hands in the green water and then splash a goodly amount of it over the cap and head of his mate, taking him totally unawares. These blokes looked local enough for me.

"How ya doin' boys?" I asked. "How did the day's play end up?" Not that I really cared, but with so many people obsessed with cricket at the moment, because of how good Bradman was, you had to keep a partial interest in it, or they'd think you were from another planet.

"We only got to see the Don make four more runs before he went out, bowled Farnes, but he'd already made 169. Australia is nine for 593. McCabe, Badcock and Gregory all made runs. McCormick and Fleetwood-Smith are still in," the lad with wet hair summarised with excitement and then had a few practice swings with his bat.

"We'd go back tomorrow, but it's a rest day. Australia can't be beaten now, can we? We'll win the series for sure. Don't you think?" asked his equally excited mate.

"Sure," I replied positively.

"One funny thing did happen today, though. Nothing to do with cricket," the wet-haired lad added.

"During lunch, a crazy bloke climbed onto the corrugated roof of the unfinished stand and unfurled a huge banner that said 'AID FOR SPAIN'. There were over eighty thousand people at the game and not one of them knew what was going on. Pamphlets began raining down on us from above; more banners appeared on the balconies as a man ran across the oval carrying a sign. It was the weirdest thing I'd ever seen, let alone at a cricket match."

Gees! These Aid for Spain people really are serious about their cause.

"Look!" the other boy jumped in "I kept a pamphlet. It's a bit crumpled, but you can read it." He carefully spread out a folded piece of paper, before handing it to me.

I flattened it out a bit more, thinking initially it might be a cricket score sheet. The message at the top of the page read:

Write your own score and help the Spanish people settle theirs.

On the other side, there was a longer message:

The Final Test

What is Bodyline compared to this?

The message continued on to explain how women and children were being slaughtered in Madrid, and how this was the first stage of a second world war.

"Can I keep the pamphlet?" I asked. "I don't think people would believe me unless they saw this. It isn't the sort of thing you expect to see at a sporting event."

"You can have it if you want. We'd better get going. We're expected back home pretty soon," replied the dry-haired lad, keen I think, to get back to talking about cricket.

"Sorry lads, one more thing. Do you blokes know of a place 'round here called the Red Square? It could be in Port."

The two young blokes looked at each other and then turned to me with strange expressions on their faces.

"Why would you wanna go there for? Too many ruffians and drunks. Just an excuse to talk poppycock, my dad says," the wet-haired lad stated, a lot less excited. "You'd be better off going to the pictures; there are always lots of girls there."

"I'll take a chance, thanks boys. How do I get there from here?" I pressed.

They told me that the coppers had moved the Red Square on from near the South Melbourne Market a month ago, down to an area of wasteland off Coventry Street, which was only about five hundred yards away on the left.

*

I could hear my destination, well before I saw it. Intermittent yelling, booing and even roars of laughter grew louder and louder, the further I went down Coventry Street. I turned right onto a large block of open land, shocked to see well over a thousand people moving around the dusty expanse. A bright light on the fascia of a hall lit up a roughly-built podium, ten yards in front.

How was it possible to entice this many people, so far out of the way?

I slowly mingled through the crowd, taking only sideways glances at the mixed bag of hard-faced men and occasional rough-looking woman that formed the majority; only a sprinkling of well-dressed types and people my own age were game enough to venture into this company. The rumbling storm clouds overhead gave the whole scene an unnatural feel, creating the impression that it was close to dark, when there had to be at least another hour of daylight left.

The focus of the crowd quickly shifted towards the makeshift podium, where a tall skinny man was striding confidently towards a rostrum, hastily lifted into position by two burly men. The skinny man wore a thick shapeless brown jacket, completely inappropriate for the heat at present, and sported a salt-and-pepper beard that came to a point in front of his green tartan tie, giving him more the appearance of an aristocrat, than the dungaree clad type I expected to front a crowd like this.

The glaring light behind the rostrum also gave the man the unexpected allure of a fire and brimstone preacher, ready to bring the wrath of God down on the unfaithful below.

The crowd roared with laughter as insults began being hurled by several rowdy groups, unwilling to wait for the speaker to commence before taking up their sport. A lot of these same blokes poured beer down their throats and then swore with a crudeness that would make wharfies blush.

"Shut up you morons! Listen to what I have to say," the thin man yelled in a broad Scottish accent.

"This country has been bled dry by greedy bloody

bosses for too long. They have no respect for what the average worker does for them. They want to send us to an early grave, while they count their profits. We need to unite, to stand up to the capitalists. And we need to do it *now!*" his voice rose to near breaking point.

"Ya look like ya never worked a day in ya bloody life, ya scrawny, pansy bastard," shouted a thickset bloke wearing an army slouch hat, his mates giving him huge pats on the back as they took long swigs from their beer bottles.

This was great!

I moved a little closer to the front.

"I will have you know that I was wounded on the Western Front in 1918, and how much compensation did I get?... *Nothing!*" the skinny man yelled again, stretching out his arms like he'd been crucified.

"I got shot in the Dardanelles, mate," another old digger shouted.

"That hurts more!" The crowd roared as the large man in the slouch hat held his crutch, digging up an old joke he knew would be a winner.

"I think he's right!" protested a young man standing behind me, silencing the loud-mouths for a second, everybody nearby taking a step back to reveal the audacious upstart.

Well! If it wasn't the angry young man from the Aid for Spain stand, without his girlfriend, Elaine, to keep him in line. He strode to within five yards of the big-mouthed interjector, pointing to the platform.

"Why don't you get up there and tell us your great plan, King Kong, instead of hiding behind your drunken mates … Well, imbecile?"

"You'd better be careful what you say, you smart little shit. We were fighting the Hun when you were still sucking on your mother," the Digger shouted in response, his mates moving as one towards the over-confident young man.

The thin man on the podium, who everyone had temporarily forgotten about, threw in his two bobs' worth in a vain attempt to save the smart-arse. "What the young man is trying to say is that …" he searched for the right words, "the government can change things to suit themselves. They can send you to a government doctor, and they'll stitch you up for good."

A lot of people in the crowd nodded in agreement, but I didn't think it would be enough to stop this young bloke getting a hiding he would never forget.

"The trouble with you old army rejects is, you were fighting the wrong enemy. Your commanders were puppets of their capitalist overlords, who profited from the death and misery of your mates," mocked the Aid for Spain worker, holding his ground as the large Anzac ran at him, his face as red as a beetroot.

I moved forward myself, to try and help this smart-aleck, for no other reasons than to return a favour and minimise the pummelling he was going to get from the rampaging bull almost on him, but I was blocked by a surging mass desperate to see some blood flow.

Through the bobbing heads of a crowd at fever pitch, many of whom had swiftly taken sides, I could make out two large figures which stepped beside and then ahead of the young man.

"*Whoa!*" the crowd groaned as a huge blow was landed on the army veteran, just before he reached his objective. The king hit delivered by a massive assailant made blood spray from the Digger's mouth as he fell back into his mate's arms, who then managed to prop him up against the woodwork of the podium. I stood mouth agape, not only at the ease of the victory, but by the fact that there were two pugilists of equally humungous size. These two near identical twins stood either side of the unflinching antagonist, their arms crossed like the boxers you might find in front of a take-on-all-comers tent at a country show, waiting to beat up a local cocky.

I thought this little kerfuffle would have satisfied the bloodlust of the crowd, but the mood only got uglier as scuffles broke out in every quarter. I decided this place was too hot for me, and it might be better to make a dignified exit without any further ado. When more mates of the Digger turned up, and started to throw bottles in the direction of the twins and their handler, I moved right out to the periphery.

Just then, a woman's shrill voice eclipsed all others.

"Gun!"

Everybody froze on the spot, eyes darting all around, trying to locate the person who could put them into the next world. No-one was sure what to do next; someone needed to take the lead.

Bang!

A loud clap of thunder cracked from directly above, making me and everyone else around me jump out of our collective skins.

I knew running wasn't the right thing to do, and something I promised myself never to do again, but I ran as fast as I could back into the shadows of Coventry Street and then as far away from the Red Square as my legs would carry me, only slowing to a walk once I had crossed over the Yarra at the Spencer Street Bridge.

*

A cold drizzly rain began to fall as I crossed over Swanston Street along Latrobe, in an almost deserted city. A shiver ran down my spine as I tried to put my long day in Emerald Hill into perspective. I was glad I had taken Lenny's advice and gone there, it really was an interesting place, and never mind some of the strange and scary incidents that occurred. It was well worth the trip but I may have to think twice about taking my sister there.

Before I turned into the quiet lane off Drummond Street that led to the rear of Aunty May's boarding house, the woman from the university sprang to mind. There was something about her that I should have noticed right from the start, and I had completely missed it. She was certainly not a professor or teacher, so how could she manage to have a small house of her own in the grounds of a university college? An ordinary worker would live outside the grounds, so there was a slim chance she was a manager of sorts.

I made up my mind that in the morning I would go back to the college to see the woman. It was the longest of all shots that she would know of work for Lettie, but it was all I had to go on at the moment. Besides, I needed to talk to her.

5

Madeline

A large black sheet-metal sign hung from a chain, strung across the same driveway that the Pom had chased me down last Wednesday night, it read in white lettering:

Entry to the University grounds is strictly prohibited to the General Public until further notice: Enquiries to the Administration Office.

Surely, this didn't have anything to do with the fight I was in the other night.

There wasn't a soul around to ask why the grounds were out of bounds, I could step over the chain and take a chance, although I didn't feel like adding trespasser to my current notoriety in the university as a brawler.

I'd put little thought into this far-fetched plan formed late last night after a very tiring day, and had stopped a dozen times on the way to the university to ask myself:

Why am I doing something so daft, when I know I'll only end up standing in front of a very puzzled woman, who'll be wondering why she ever bothered helping a young fool with more front than Myers?

One thing I did plan to do before I got into the grounds, was to avoid being recognised by anyone that had a ring-side seat from the second floor window on the night of the fight, one of whom I knew was a professor. I had decided to don a cap for the day, which had Aunty May giving me funnier looks than usual because she knows I rarely wear a hat, even on the hottest of days.

Before I turned around to head back home dejected, it occurred to me that I had made it out of the grounds via a path on Wednesday night, so why couldn't I get back in the same way. The trouble was, everything looked completely different in broad daylight, compared to the darkness of that night. So, I didn't have much hope of finding it now.

Bugger it! I'm going in this way.

I took a quick look around, before stepping over the chain and then walking at a brisk pace down the drive, hoping like hell I didn't run into anybody. After a hundred yards, where the road started to curve, I turned right onto a paved pathway, where I could see another hundred yards ahead, the same small building I had been given refuge in.

"May we help you?" a cultured voice asked me from behind.

I swung around to see three prim and proper students in green and white jackets, embroidered with insignia.

Prefects! ... They had to be.

The tallest student stepped forward, without saying a word.

"I'm just going to visit the lady who lives in the building down the path, to ask about work for my sister," I replied, trying to think fast on my feet. "My aunt knows her."

"Does she now?" the tallest prefect replied, with a smug grin on his face. "Then, what is the name of the lady in the building, and what is your aunt's name?" After a second he added "And, may I ask what your name is?"

"I'm not telling you my name, or my aunt's name, and I already told you, she knows her," I shot back angrily, getting browned off, straight up, by this uppity bastard, and by the fact that I should have asked the woman's name on Wednesday night.

"I'm not satisfied with the reason you're sneaking around the grounds of our college," the tallest prefect stated in an accusatory tone, before whispering something into the shortest prefect's ear.

His lackey, then bolted towards the main college buildings, with my luck to get the professor who saw me in the fight last Wednesday night.

Now, I was getting annoyed. These blokes had me pegged as a lowlife thief, or worse.

"Listen here," I insisted, the Irish rising in my voice. "I'm no bloody thief. I just wanted to ask the woman, that my aunt does know, if she's heard of any work 'round here that might be suitable for my sister, who's arriving down from the country on Tuesday. I thought the lady might ..." I stopped, seeing only blank expressions on the students' faces.

"It was a long shot. That's all."

"You should go now," said the tallest of the students. "You can leave the same way as you came in. If you would like to make an appointment to visit the lady concerned, you can arrange it through our Administration Department during office hours, Monday to Friday. Then we can escort you through the grounds to see her after that."

"But, I'm almost there," I exclaimed, surprised by their officiousness.

"Why can't you escort me now?"

"Are you not aware that there is an infantile paralysis epidemic spreading throughout the area?" the tallest prefect responded sharply, looking down on me as if I was an idiot. "The grounds have been closed to prevent the disease spreading from the public to the students."

I stood in silence looking at the two students, understanding that they were right. I shouldn't have just barged into the grounds. Hell, I might be spreading the disease right now and not even know it. Aunty May had told me how bad polio was but I hadn't taken much notice of her.

The shorter prefect who had been quiet up until now, piped up, "She's not in now anyway ... she's visiting her daughter at the Children's."

The tallest prefect turned around immediately, giving him a look that could kill.

*

I returned to Aunty May's for Sunday lunch, I had no choice, but I was determined to get back to the college as soon as possible while there was still a slim chance of catching the woman on her way back from the Children's Hospital.

Another reason I needed to return quickly, was that I had no way of complying with the requirements given to me by the prefects to arrange an appointment through the Administration Department, my 'office' hours far exceeded those of the University's.

On returning, I slumped against the brick outer wall of the King's College, taking advantage of the shade provided by a large river red gum, expecting a long wait ahead for a person that was possibly in the grounds already, and that I might be better off not seeing, anyway. I was upset by the revelation that this woman had a sick child and devastated to think that I may have caused it.

After more than an hour, I caught a glimpse of a woman in a blue hat and dress making her way around the slight curve of the College Crescent; a woman that I had been beginning to think was a figment of my imagination.

I felt a certain amount of dread at seeing her again, considering what I may have put her through, but then came a surge of relief.

As the woman drew nearer a smile appeared on her face.

"Sebastian, how are you?" she asked on reaching me. "It's Madeline ... My name is Madeline. I should have told you last Wednesday night."

Madeline then leant forward and kissed me on the cheek. Her skin was soft against mine, with a faint scent of spice in her perfume, stepping back to look at my shocked face.

"Don't worry, Sebastian. You won't have to marry me!" Madeline added with a wry grin. "I'm already married."

I had not expected this. Instantly, I saw her as someone different to the woman that had helped me, only a few days before.

"Come along with me, Sebastian, I'll show you how to avoid being seen by the snitches."

Madeline turned and walked down to a wall of greenery just before the main drive, and then pushed a concealed gate that opened into the grounds.

"Well, are you coming?" Madeline asked. "I have something I need to ask you."

I followed Madeline along an overgrown, ivy-covered path, with so many twists and turns it made me wonder how I ever found my way last time.

"I was so worried about you after the fight, Sebastian. Were you fine the next day?" Madeline asked as the path opened onto the rear of her house.

"I got a bit of a hurry-up from my foreman at work that morning, but in the end he let me go home early, which was a first. My aunt wasn't happy either, so I copped it for a couple of days, but it could 'a been worse. I've also managed to avoid running into my Pommy friend and his mates, so far,"

"Have you done anything else since then?" Madeline asked, while I held open the flyscreen door for her to unlock the main wooden door.

"Come in, Sebastian."

I hesitated for a second, unsure if this was the right place to be.

"You are more than welcome," Madeline assured me, holding the main door open. "Besides, you've been here before."

On entering the kitchen and looking around trying to familiarise myself again, I remembered that Madeline had asked me a question.

"Sorry, yeah. Yesterday, I went to South Melbourne. It's quite a place!"

"It is a nice place, the shopping is always good there," Madeline nodded in agreement, before removing her pixie-like, blue gorra hat.

She was younger and prettier than I recalled, shapely in an aqua-blue dress, her mousy hair was pulled back tightly from her scalp, finishing in a bun; a few strands of hair still managing to fly free in front of her forehead.

"I should explain why I asked you to come back to my house, Sebastian. But first, come into the lounge and make yourself comfortable. I'll make a pot of tea for us."

Madeline moved an old blanket from her couch and asked me if I would like to sit down. I sat on the edge of the leather, still surprised at being back in her digs again.

She stood in the doorway and must have noticed my discomfort. "I was informed by senior undergraduates from this college that a young man came into the grounds looking for me this morning. They thought it may have been a pretext for skulduggery, although the young man swore he was only in the grounds on behalf of his sister."

Madeline shot me a quizzical look.

"I didn't think they believed me." I added.

She left to go and make the tea, leaving me completely on the edge of my seat. I wanted to ask about her daughter and selfishly how she became ill. But, decided quickly not to say a word, it might be too painful a subject to touch on. And, I was surprised she was married, I had no inkling of that the other night.

"I have a few questions I'd like to ask you, Sebastian," Madeline declared on returning from the kitchen, placing a cup of tea, and scones on the low table in front of me. "But before that, the seniors did mention your sister was looking for work. She is obviously moving down to Melbourne, so you must be excited about that. I hope all the other news from home has been good?"

"Pretty good," I began, and then knew I had to be honest, "A mixed bag really. Lettie, I mean Leticia, will put a positive spin on it, I'm sure."

Madeline's eyes never left mine as she sat down at the other end of the couch, before asking in a serious tone, "Sebastian, do you know a young man called William, he's a senior undergraduate from the King's College?"

"No, not at all," I replied, shaking my head.

"I am not permitted to tell you his full name, but he says he knows you."

I looked up at Madeline gobsmacked, trying to think of anyone I knew called William.

"Honestly, I don't know any William at all, never mind from a university. He must be mistaken."

"I have only spoken to him a few times before in the dining room. He is quite an arrogant character. I was surprised when he knocked on my door, only an hour after the three seniors had left me. He said I should consider helping your sister find work because you had inspired him in the past ... he wouldn't tell me how."

"Inspired?" I repeated quickly.

I jumped up and walked around the room before returning to sit on the couch, looking at Madeline to try and gauge what she was thinking.

"I told him I had been let down too many times in the past by helping people, so I had no intention of being let down again. He became quite agitated by my refusal and stormed off."

"This bloke can't go around saying he knows me, I need to front him."

"The university doesn't need any more confrontations at the moment, Sebastian, so it may be best to let this pass. I will make a report if he returns again."

There was silence for a moment before Madeline asked me exactly why I had come to the college to see her. I told her that my parents had written to my aunt, believing it would be best for my sister if she had a change of surrounds, and that meant moving down to the city to find work.

"My sister Lettie is a great girl, a lot of fun, almost all the time. To be quite honest, I'm not completely sure why she's coming down to Melbourne, but I was hoping to surprise her with the prospect of a job, to get her off on the right foot. I can tell you no one works as hard as she does."

Madeline's eyes were down, which I took as a bad sign, until I said:

"She's also a great cook, if that's of any use."

Madeline looked up and then slowly straightened on the couch.

"Did you know I was the manager of the college kitchen before you came to visit me this morning or was it just a wild guess?"

"I didn't know what you did here. I just had a hunch you might have some pull around the place."

I felt a lot better that I could talk freely to Madeline about the reason why I came to see her. I probably should have left it at that.

"Unfortunately, I did a good job of embarrassing myself by ignoring the sign across the driveway that said no-one was allowed in."

"One of the seniors told me that you appeared shocked, when he mentioned that I was visiting my daughter at the Children's Hospital. He shouldn't have said anything, but since he has... I want to tell you there is no reason to be alarmed. My daughter does have polio, Sebastian, but she is doing well and has plenty of friends and lots of support in the hospital. She contracted it a year ago, at roughly the same time my husband felt he should look for work interstate."

"He's not a strong man," Madeline said quietly, suddenly looking drawn, before quickly steadying herself.

"Sorry. Things became difficult between us as soon as we moved down from Sydney, six years ago. He couldn't find work, but I managed to luckily, in the kitchen of the King's College. The last time I heard from my husband, he was in Queensland. He wrote that he wanted to stay on for a short while after the cane harvest, saying he would be back down in two months ... that was eight months ago. I want to apologise for not asking you to stay longer on Wednesday night, Sebastian. I was concerned you may be found here. I hope you can forgive me."

"You don't ever have to apologise to me for anything, Madeline. I was just glad you didn't lag me into the coppers, or worse, the professor."

She gave me a tiny smile as she picked up my empty cup and saucer, an indication that it was time for me to leave. At the kitchen door, Madeline stopped and looked back at me.

"The last of the boarders are due to return within a week, that's when the kitchen needs all hands on deck. It's hot, heavy work, and I don't put up with shirkers. Bring your sister around to the front of my house at two o'clock, next Saturday afternoon. I will let the seniors know you will be escorting her into the grounds. We will be catering the tutors' welcoming dinner, which usually finishes late so I would recommend that Leticia be picked up afterwards."

Madeline then made sure I had her full attention.

"... and Sebastian. Leticia will only get one chance to impress."

"Don't worry, she's a breath of fresh air," I said positively, trying to dispel any doubt. "You'll see!"

"I will."

I took my cue to leave and Madeline saw me out the screen door, leaving me to make my own way along the secluded path and out of the grounds.

Once again, I forgot to say 'thank you' to this incredibly generous woman.

6

Lettie Arrives

Aunty May was particularly quiet as she sipped on her nectar tea. We were waiting in a small café off the main hall of Spencer Street Station for Lettie's train to arrive. I'd resolved to enjoy the peace as things may not be this quiet for too much longer, especially if Aunty May tried to tell Lettie how to dress and act down here. I wouldn't necessarily call Lettie stubborn, bossy sometimes, yes, but she certainly wouldn't back down if she thought she was in the right.

I was enjoying the quiet that moment for another reason; after I saw Madeline on Sunday afternoon my head had felt like it had been split by a mattock. I had over-taxed my brain trying to figure out who this mystery senior could be, and also, what to make of my somewhat unsettling visit which I really hoped would turn out to be a good thing for Lettie.

I decided on Sunday night not to let Aunty May in on the news of the job trial and how I had gone to a university college twice, only to end up in a woman's house. I don't know how I could have explained that.

I knew telling the truth was always the best policy, but when things were as complicated as this, it was perhaps the best policy to keep Aunty May out of the picture for as long as possible; as long as possible that is, when dealing with a natural busybody. So, I would definitely be taking Lettie aside, to tell her the good news about the opportunity in Madeline's kitchen.

As far as the rest of the whole, sometimes, sorry story was concerned I'd have to be straight up with Lettie, maybe leaving out the bit about Madeline kissing me on the cheek when I met her Sunday afternoon.

Excitement spread throughout the friends and relatives waiting in the main hall, as news of the Adelaide train's arrival was announced over the newly installed public address system. At least twenty past eight in the evening was a civilised-enough time for us to find Lettie and then catch her favourite, the cable trolley-tram back to Aunty May's, in time to have some tea and scones for supper.

On the Country Arrivals platform, Aunty May wasn't enjoying being knocked from pillar to post by the jostling crowd. We craned our necks, searching up and down the length of the jam-packed train, for Lettie to appear out of the swirling steam. Through a sea of waving hats and hands, I caught a glimpse of Lettie coming out of a carriage door backwards, a fair way down the platform; she seemed to be talking to someone inside.

Lettie had finally arrived.

I pointed her out to Aunty May, who started huffing about how far away she was. I could see Lettie being handed a large suitcase and a Gladstone bag by an elderly gentleman, which I presumed she placed on the platform, before returning to help the gentleman out of the carriage. Typical Lettie, I thought, making a lifelong friend in a few hours. But, when she started helping the elderly gentleman along the platform while carrying his large suitcase, it occurred to me, where the hell was her luggage?

Aunty May was aware of what she had done as well and pushed me in the back.

"Quick, Sebastian! Go down and get her luggage before some shyster picks them up. They're always hanging around here. Quick!"

I ran as fast as I could, dodging people and luggage, along the platform towards Lettie, who was still helping the elderly gentleman along. As soon as she saw me, she dropped the old man's suitcase like a hot potato and then ran towards me jumping up and yelling like a mad thing, her arms wide open for me to give her a big hug.

"How the hell are ya, Grub?" Lettie yelled. "Good, I hope?" she said, squeezing the air out of me, "I'm so glad to be here."

"I'm great, Lett," I choked out. "Lett, where's ya luggage?"

"I left it back on the platform, Grub," Lettie replied, with a surprised look on her face. "I was gonna go back and get 'em after I took the old bloke out the front. They'll be right."

"No, they won't, Lett. There're all sorts of bodgies hangin' round the station, just waitin' to snatch loose luggage like yours."

"Righto, Grub, since you've turned into a worry wart, you take the old fella and his suitcase out, I'll go back and get my stuff. His name is Stan, and he's a real funny bugger ... smells a bit though."

Hell's bells! Lettie's going to have to smarten herself up real quick, if she wants to make it down here. I don't want her to have to learn things the hard way.

When we turned around to get the old timer, he was gone, nowhere to be seen.

"Oh, well. He couldn't have needed that much help," I shrugged.

Lettie held tightly onto my arm during our walk back to where she had left her luggage, happier than I thought she would be, to be away from home.

"How's the old battle-axe treatin' ya Grubby, stickin' her nose into ya business is she?" Lettie asked as she pointed out two small canvas bags, luckily still where she left them.

"She's all right, Lett. Ya just gotta keep out of her way, all the time," I grinned before I leant down to pick up both bags. "Is that all of your luggage, Lett. I thought you'd have more?"

"Give me one. I'll tell ya 'bout it later," Lettie replied

quietly, shaking her head "I'll tell ya 'bout everything later."

"We better get back to the old dragon, before she has a turn or something, Grub. Suppose ya heard about Dad's truck hey, real bloody mess that was. The folks won't listen, ya know."

Lettie remained surprisingly quiet while we walked back to join Aunty May, her seriousness starting to worry me.

"Lett, don't say anything in front of Aunty May, but I've got some ripper news for ya. I'm sure you'll like it."

"Now I'm worried," Lettie said, forcing a smile to show me her old self was still in there.

When we reached Aunty May, she appeared genuinely happy to see Lettie, and I could even see a small tear in the corner of her eye, as she was given the same big hug as me. A cold draught that had managed to enter the main hall helped us make up our minds to head for home and a warm cup of tea. After we left the station onto a windswept Spencer Street, rain spitting, Aunty May and Lettie declared, almost in unison.

"There is no way we are going up front on a cable tram dummy, on a night like tonight."

I had nothing to argue with, so we headed across the road to try and find a new tram heading up Bourke Street. But, as luck would have it, a cable tram just started coming out of its Spencer Street depot.

All of a sudden Aunty May lifted her arm, waving

down the gripman. "All right, Sebastian, this will save us waiting, but I'm getting in the trailer," Aunty May insisted, "Leticia, can make up her own mind, if she wants to join me or not."

Lettie did the right thing and stayed with Aunty May in the trailer, allowing a chance for them to catch up on their own. I sat alone facing a biting wind at the front of the cable tram dummy, unable to recall a better trip, the way ahead looked decidedly on the up.

The only slight downside to our trip, was that cable trams no longer ran up Rathdowne Street. The closest stop to Aunty May's now was along Nicholson, opposite the Exhibition Building.

Fortunately, the rain cleared, and a warm breeze blew in during our walk across Carlton Gardens. Lettie and I began reminiscing about the endless hours we spent there as kids, making up the silliest of games to keep ourselves amused. We waited until Aunty May was out of earshot, before we made a plan to catch up tomorrow after I got home from work.

By the time we reached Aunty May's, everybody had given up on the idea of tea and scones; we all needed our beds too much. There would be plenty of time for news, good or bad, tomorrow.

*

The first thing I noticed out of the ordinary, was a pair of girl's legs tapping away on the cobblestones in the lane behind Aunty May's, as I trudged the last fifty yards home from work.

It was Lettie waiting on the back steps wearing a thin, plain cotton dress, barely enough for this coolish day. A teapot, a milk jug, cups and a plateful of scones placed on the step beside.

"Cuppa, Grub?" Lettie asked, with a Cheshire cat smile on her face. A smile I was glad to see, after getting a feeling that the news from home may not be that good.

"Thanks, Lett. You're a life saver. This tannery work is for mugs, ya know."

I sat down on the step behind Lettie and then leant back against the screen door, wondering if it would be best to tell her my news now, or wait until later, when Lettie and I may need some good news to cheer us up.

"Tell us ya news, Grub. I'll let ya know if it's a ripper or not. Ya still take milk don't ya?"

"Lett," I hesitated for a second, "I got a trial for a job for ya at the Melbourne Uni on Saturday. You'll be working in the kitchen of the King's College."

Lettie looked at me as if I didn't know her at all, or what was happening to her at the moment.

"I do appreciate what you've done, but I have to talk to ya about what we're gonna do about home first. Things are so confused back there. I can't tell ya how much."

Lettie handed me my cuppa and then passed me a scone.

"Dad's truck didn't catch on fire, Grub." Lettie was struggling to get the words out "He set fire to it."

I sat silently looking into my cup, not expecting that piece of news.

"Why?" I asked, turning to look at Lettie. "He's all right isn't he?"

"He's not thinkin' right for a start. That's for sure. He burnt his right arm trying to put the fire out, when the truck was past saving. Tiny had to pull him away. He burnt his arm as well. Dad ended up in the hospital for two days, Mum's been watching over him at home ever since."

"The trouble is, Dad thinks Robbie is a genius and wants to send him to a university. That's why he burnt the truck, to get the insurance money. Robbie is clever, no-one can argue with that, but now, all he does is memorise every piece of rubbish he comes across and then repeats it out loud, no matter where he is. I don't know what people think of him. He also gets so violent if you try to take him away from his books, and luckily for all of us, he still wants to go to school. I hate to say it, Grub. But, I think there's something seriously wrong with him."

I stood up and threw my scone away, watching it shatter on the paling fence opposite.

"Sorry, Lett," I apologised while I walked a few steps

into the lane. "I kind 'a thought this might happen one day. If the doctors get hold of him, they'll throw him in the asylum. I won't have him in there, the stories I've heard about what goes on inside are horrendous."

"Ya know, Dad spends most of his time now staring out the window, waiting for news from the insurance company," Lettie explained, then had a sip of her tea, "He mightn't get any money at all, they say. Lots of places have been torched lately, even the old toy factory in town. The insurance companies are sending up inspectors from the city to check on their local assessors so anything could happen."

I came back and sat on the step, wishing I didn't feel so helpless. I couldn't even send up some money.

"Tiny has been fantastic. He works at the hardware store during the day and then goes home and does what he can. The stupid part is, the truck was doin' really well. Dad did panic a bit when the fuel distributor wanted him to put more money on his account. He just hasn't thought anything through clearly for a long time now, Grub. Neither has Mum really, she agrees with any nonsense he comes up with. I just ended up arguing with them both."

"Lett, I don't know what to do, I don't. If I go back, I'll only end up getting in the way, becoming a burden on them unless I have some whiz-bang job to go back to."

"Maybe, they should just sell the farm and move into town, they might get a fair price."

"No-one's bought a farm around there for years, ya know that," Lettie replied, stretching out her legs as if she had more to say. "I had to get away. I quit my job at the drapers to help Mum, but I felt like a third wheel all day. So, I asked Mum and Dad if they would write to Aunty May, to see if I could come down, but now I'm here ... I wanna go back home."

Lettie has taken the brunt of what's happened back home — and most of it to heart. It's not fair on her at all, but I couldn't come up with a single decent idea that would make it better.

"Lett, listen. If we both had jobs, we could send money back to Tiny; he'll put it to good use."

"Tell me about this job at the uni," Lettie asked, both of us ready to change the subject "You said it was in a kitchen, didn't ya? What do I have to do?"

"I don't know for sure, Lett, but I told the manageress there you could cook really well and she sounded interested. She said the kitchen was catering a tutors' dinner on Saturday night and it could go late."

"How do ya know a manageress from a fancy college, Grub? By the smell of ya, she might think you're a lamb and throw ya in a pot. Go on tell me how ya know her, or else I'll bang on ya door in the middle of the night till ya do."

Thankfully, Lettie was back to her cheery old self again. I couldn't take it if she was down all the time.

"Ya won't have to do that, Lett. I met her after I got into a fight with a local thug from around the corner who chased me into the uni. Thankfully, the kitchen manageress hid me until I could get away and make it home. I went to see her at the university on Sunday to say thanks and then she said she needed help in the kitchen next Saturday. So, I said you could cook, which she was impressed with and then she said she would give you a trial. She's a nice lady, her name is Madeline."

Lettie was quiet, trying to figure out if I was pulling her leg.

"It's true Lett, don't ask me exactly what you'll be doing. I just don't know. She really is a nice lady though, you'll find out."

Bloody hell! What more can I do?

"Righto, Grub. At the moment, I'll say I'll give it a go. But, I could change my mind, depending on what we decide about home." Then, after a second, "Do I need to bring anything?"

"Just ya good self, Lett. Madeline said I have to take ya to her place in the grounds, 'cause of a bad polio outbreak nearby."

"They've been testing kids in the country too. The doctors even thought Robbie might have it. Something showed up on his lungs on the first test, but nothing was there when he was tested again. It took one hell of an effort to get him tested twice, I can tell ya."

"I haven't told Aunty May anything about the job, Lett, or anything for that matter about what happened at the uni, and I definitely don't want her to know about Madeline. She would do her 'nana'. I don't know if I should let her in on part of the story. What d'ya reckon, Lett?"

"Don't tell her anything, Grub," Lettie replied, nonchalantly. "Mightn't get the job anyway. We can tell her later on."

"Tell who later on, Leticia?"

Aunty May had appeared out of nowhere, dressed in a smart mauve dress, sporting her favourite fox pelt stole. I don't know how long she had been standing behind us.

"No-one Aunty. You look splendid tonight, don't you?" Lettie replied, putting on a surprisingly good cultured accent. "Are you going out?"

"Yes, as a matter of fact. Barry is taking me to the Crystal Café for dinner. I believe it is the place to be in Melbourne at the moment."

Just then my foreman appeared on the back steps, looking silly in an overly tight suit. I could barely contain my laughter while he introduced himself to Lettie, before Aunty May took his arm and they headed off towards Lygon Street.

"Have a swell night," Lettie yelled out, making them both turn around and wave.

"Who's that wowser, not another shifty bugger, I hope?"

"He's my foreman at work, Lett," I replied, less than enthusiastically.

"Couldn't lay straight in bed."

We chatted for ages after Aunty May and Barry had gone, talking about all the gossip back home. Lettie described how Tiny had tried to set her up with one of his good mates at a local dance, only to end in disaster, when his mate got roaring drunk. She also told me my mate Arty had been back in town for two weeks and had come out to the farm to let the family know he and his dad had bought a farm in New South Wales for nicks, and wouldn't be back down that way for a long time.

By the time it was too dark to sit out the back, I had managed to polish off enough scones to do me for tea. It was a good feeling having my best mate in town.

*

Lettie struggled to settle in for the first few days. The room she was given, next to Aunty May's, stank more than I remembered, probably due to the fact it had belonged to a heavy drinker for several years and the sash window only opened up a couple of inches to let in fresh air.

I had never seen Lettie as nervous about anything in her life as she was about her job trial on Saturday. She threatened several times not to go, saying she felt like she was abandoning her family by being down here, and daily wanted to go home. She knew going home was impossible, for the simple fact she didn't have enough money for the return train trip, and there was no way Aunty May would give it to her.

By Friday, Lettie had come around, telling Aunty May she was going for a long walk on her own around the Carlton area, to visit some of the old haunts we used to hang around as kids, and maybe dropping in at Melbourne University to see if there was any work. Aunty May said she was wasting her time at the university, and wasn't happy she was wandering off at a time when there was such a worry about the polio epidemic and so many unemployed people 'of dubious character' hanging around on street corners.

I was proud Lettie had taken it on her own bat, to try and see Madeline at the King's College kitchen, to introduce herself before her trial on Saturday. She did the right thing, unlike me, by going to the University Administration Office, only to be told by some snooty secretary that there was no way the kitchen manageress could be disturbed at that time, and all applications for college positions were exclusively requested in writing, so she must be mistaken about the job.

When I caught up with Lettie on Friday evening, she was nervous all over again, asking me time and time again whether I was sure the job trial was legitimate, as she had already told Aunty May about being given a try out for tomorrow. So, if it wasn't on the up and up, she would never speak to me again.

My main worry though was the mystery senior. I had to tell Lettie about him, especially as he claimed to know me and also knew Lettie may be given a chance by Madeline in the college kitchen. I had to tell Lettie the whole truth about everything that had happened lately.

*

We were late to head off to the university on Saturday afternoon after the foreman made me stay back and help unload a dray full of skins. I was near exhaustion, after I ran home and then gave myself a quick wash under the arms, before putting on some decent clobber for the afternoon.

Aunty May did wish Lettie the best of luck as we headed off, and thankfully didn't ask too many questions about how she got a trial, when so many others couldn't get a foot in the prestigious doors.

By the time we had reached the Swanston Street perimeter of the university, Lettie had been filled in on my eventful last ten days. Fortunately, none of the stories affected the spring in her step.

"You've been a busy boy, Grub. Ya must a' been cackin' your pants when the big Pom chased ya into the college. I bet ya never thought ya'd be headin' back this way again with me, on my way to try out for a job with the woman that saved ya bacon," Lettie giggled, excited and much happier I had been honest with her.

"What ya said about that prefect-type saying that he knows ya and telling Madeline she should help me out with a job. That scares me a bit. No-one we know has gone on to university. He must be barkin' mad this bloke."

I am not so sure about that!

The closer we got to the King's College the less assured Lettie became, complaining that her clothes were too old and drab for a trial, and sure they would cook exotic dishes in the kitchen, not the plain farm food she cooked back home. When we reached the chain across the driveway at the side entrance to the King's College we stopped, like it was a massive wall between two worlds.

"Righto, Lett. Let's see if I'm really leadin' ya up the garden path," I joked, before we stepped over the chain together and headed towards Madeline's house, hoping I really wasn't.

No-one stopped us this time, as we walked under a high canopy of oak trees filtering the sun and protecting us from a blustery wind. Lettie held tightly onto my arm, while we slowly walked the final fifty yards to the front of Madeline's house.

I knocked on the door, the same as I had on the Wednesday before last, with a real anticipation that this was going to work out well for Lettie. We could hear movement inside, expecting Madeline to open the door any second. When the door failed to open after a minute,

Lettie's fidgeting became worse. Yet, we could still hear banging noises coming from inside.

Then we heard a girl's faint voice.

"Wait, please ... I've nearly got it open."

Lettie looked at me with concern. We could see the doorknob turning back and forth repeatedly. The next second the door flew inwards, revealing a young girl in a wheelchair in the doorway.

"Hello, my name is Bernadette. My mum's not here now, she's gone to the kitchen," explained the blonde, curly-haired girl.

"Hello, lovely to meet you, Bernadette. We were to meet your mum here, but if you could point out where the kitchen is, we could meet her there," Lettie asked, with the biggest smile on her face, relieved at seeing this adorable little girl.

The girl manoeuvred her wheelchair around until she was satisfied the right building was in sight.

"My mum is over there," pointing between us, to a building at the far end of the grounds.

I guarantee Lettie would spoil this girl silly, if she ever got to spend any time with her.

"My dad will be here in two weeks. Do you know him?" the little girl asked, with real excitement in her eyes.

I got such a deflated feeling to hear her bludger of a father was coming back, but I replied cheerily, "No, we don't, Bernadette. But, I may have a word with him when he comes down. We better go now, righto. Nice to meet you, and make sure to close the door behind us."

"Bye," Lettie said, giving little waves to Bernadette as we left.

Lettie and I smiled at each other, as we headed in a roundabout way towards where Bernadette had pointed, trying not to leave the pathway in case we ruffled the feathers of some gardener.

We walked in amazement past the castle-like main hall of the King's College, feeling like we really were in a different world. There was certainly something powerful about this place, although I couldn't quite put my finger on it.

In the distance, I could make out a cream delivery van with its rear doors open, parked to the side of a smaller college building, a man lumping large white bags, probably flour, through an open screen door.

"That'll be the kitchen," I told Lettie.

We walked as fast as we could, as if the kitchen might vanish if we didn't get there quick enough.

When we reached what I was certain was the college kitchen, I called out to the delivery man, who was just about to go through the open door. He almost fell flat on his face trying to halt the momentum of the heavy bags of flour on his shoulders.

"Sorry, mate," I apologised, at seeing the man turning red in the face, while placing the bags of flour on the ground. I reckon if we weren't in earshot of the kitchen, I would have got a mouthful.

"Do you know a lady called Madeline?" I asked. "She's the manageress of the kitchen."

"Yeah, she's inside. I'll get her for ya." He stared at me. "And don't ever stop a loaded man like that again, mate. Consider ya-self lucky I'm a gentleman, and I'm on my last drop for the week."

We had waited three or four minutes at the screen door, before Madeline appeared, flushed in the face and dressed in a light pink uniform, dusted with flour.

"Hello, there! I see you've found our humble kitchen. I'm Madeline, so glad you came," Madeline wiped her hands free of flour before she shook Lettie's hand. "Now, shall I call you Leticia, or would you prefer Lettie?"

"Lettie is just fine, thanks, and thanks for giving me a chance," Lettie replied politely. "And your daughter is beautiful."

"That she is Lettie," Madeline returned, before quickly changing the subject. "You may wish I hadn't given you a trial by the end of the night. We have a big task ahead of us."

"And how are you, Sebastian, keeping out of trouble?" smiled Madeline.

"I'm trying my best, but my record around here isn't good," I replied with a grin. "I'm happy you've finally got to meet my sister."

"Okay, enough with the pleasantries, time for work. Come along with me, Lettie. I think I have a uniform in your size." Then, Madeline looked at me again.

"Sebastian, Lettie will see you out front of the main college drive at around ten. Actually, come a little earlier, in case they don't like the sponge," Madeline chuckled, as she showed Lettie into the kitchen.

I stepped back over the chain in the driveway again feeling positive that Lettie would do well tonight. Selfishly, I didn't want her to go back home and I really believed she didn't either.

At the end of the driveway, I was about to turn onto the footpath that would take me back to Aunty May's, when I noticed someone out of the corner of my eye.

"Hello," called out a man's voice. "Nice to see you again!"

I turned to see a young man, dressed smartly in a green and white senior's jacket, leaning against the college wall. I had to look twice before I realised who it was. It was the smart-aleck from the Aid for Spain stand.

"May I introduce myself properly, Sebastian? My name is William Reinecke," then, after a second, "You can call me Bill, when you get to know me better."

7

The Sometimes 'Prefect'

The senior pushed off from the college wall, messing up his neatly combed black hair until it resembled the wild curly mess I remembered from the Aid for Spain stand.

"I fear we may have got off on the wrong foot, Sebastian. So, I have prepared an interesting afternoon's entertainment for you. I think you will enjoy it. We can get to know each other better." I was too surprised to speak. "Well, come along, then!" he demanded.

"I'm not going anywhere with you, you smart shit," I snapped back. "I ought 'a punch ya in the bloody face!"

I looked around quickly to see if his two massive guard dogs were anywhere in the vicinity, hiding in wait, ready to jump to his aid. This William fellow was bigger and taller than me but, if nothing else, I would make sure I had landed one good punch on him before he got me.

"Now, now, Sebastian, let's be civil," William said calmly. "And if you're looking for my brothers in arms, they are in the country fighting in a boxing tournament. Under the same name, I'm told. Quite a scam, if it works."

"I don't care what they're doin'," I shot back. "Who the hell are you?"

This bloke was as mad as a hatter and I didn't need to be around people like that.

"I must insist we get going, Sebastian," William said impatiently as he started to stroll towards the city. "What I have to show you is important. It won't wait."

"What I can't wait for, is for you to apologise to me. I don't know what kind of fantasy world you're living in, where you think you can get away with screaming at people you don't know and then letting your thugs loose on old Diggers. But I don't wanna know about it."

William stopped and then turned around sharply, not seeming to take my rebuke well.

"My apologies, Sebastian, but I thought you may have appreciated that I helped when you were in a little strife with your large English friend. If you put a little trust in me, everything will be explained to your satisfaction."

He started off again towards the city, this time at a steady pace. Not for the first time, I was stumped to know what to do. This bloke was so full of himself, it beggared belief. He acted like a champion of war victims one day and then a pretentious college student the next.

I was put in a huge bind here. Lettie's whole future in the college could be jeopardised by this show pony. I hate acting like a sheep, following the mob, but I had to find out what this poser was up to.

He said 'put a little trust in me'. I'd start off with the tiniest 'little'.

I started to walk in the direction of the city, keeping William in sight, but in no real hurry to catch up to this strange character, although I was more than a little curious to find out what had made him tell Madeline I was inspiring to him.

He stopped to wait for me outside the City Baths, this time leaning against one of the pillars that formed the entrance steps.

"Do you know what I like about you, Sebastian?" he said, when I finally caught up with him.

"Even after I was extremely rude to you last Saturday afternoon, you still bought something from Elaine to help the Spanish cause. It takes a strong person to do that. While you were being beaten to a pulp by the exceptionally large Englishman, I always had confidence you would overcome him," he said with a wry smile that meant he had no confidence I could beat the Englishman, "but as it offered up such a unique opportunity for me to right some wrongs, I couldn't refuse to act. And you did move to come to my aid at the Red Square ... that was inspirational to me.

"By the way, Sebastian, the said Englishman has left the country, back to the 'Old Dart'. His Irish friend with the sore ear appears to have disappeared without a trace."

I went over again what he had just said, not believing what I was hearing.

"The owner of the Magenta Club, a fine Jewish gentleman from Sydney, is a generous supporter of the Aid for Spain campaign. Apparently, the two men in question were meant to be looking after his ladies, but instead, were more concerned with selling their not-so-kosher goods to passers-by on Lygon Street and randomly harassing others."

Holy Moses, this know-all does know everything.

"By the way, Sebastian, may I ask what your sister's name is?"

Or does he?

"Ya can keep my sister out of this," I replied, sharply. "I mean it. I don't want ya goin' anywhere near her in the college. If ya want to find out her name. I'm sure a know-all like you could figure it out."

"A 'know-all like me', is it Sebastian?"

William took a step towards me, I knew I'd hit a raw nerve. He came close up to my face, glaring into my eyes, trying to dominate me with his anger. I needed to use all the fortitude I had, to stand my ground and not turn away from his stare. I wasn't going to give this overblown schoolboy the satisfaction of having anything over me. After what seemed like an eternity he nodded his head, seemingly satisfied with the outcome of his little game, still not prepared to avert his eyes.

"Well done, Sebastian. Most people can't look me straight in the eye."

We reached Swanston Street. Like most Saturday after-noons it was teeming with people, today more so, probably due to the return of mild weather. William stopped on the corner of Swanston and Collins looking around at all and sundry and then for a long time up Collins Street, oblivious to me for close to two minutes, before appearing satisfied with whatever he was looking at.

"Sebastian, I think we should go to the cinema ... the flicks."

William's voice had changed from posh upper-crust to something like a working man's, in mid-sentence. He pointed to the Regent Theatre and that's where he headed.

"I was plannin' to go to the flicks tomorra' with my sister. She might wanna see the same show," I yelled out, but I don't think he heard, or wanted to hear me, because he continued to walk fearlessly through a full line of traffic towards the Regent.

I caught up with this sometimes 'prefect' out front of the Regent Theatre, expecting to go up the stairs into the magnificent foyer.

"You won't be watchin' the same show, Seb. Can I call ya Seb, Sebastian?" then, slipping back into his posh self again, "Come along with me."

William and I had walked only a short distance up Collins Street before we stopped at a plain door marked 'Stage Door'.

"Wait here," William demanded and then walked back

down towards the main entrance, turning left to go inside.

After twenty minutes or so had ticked by, I was beginning to feel like a shag on a rock, hanging around outside the Stage Door. The few people that came and went through it must have wondered if I was slightly touched waiting for actors that never get to leave the silver screen.

That was when I thought, *this smarty is playing a bloody trick on me.*

I didn't know him from Adam. This could be some long-winded joke he'd worked out to make me pay for what I said at the Aid for Spain stand. He's most likely laughing himself silly inside the theatre with Elaine trying to stop him.

I'd give him a couple more minutes and then I'd be off. *Why did I ever follow this bloke into town?*

The Stage Door suddenly opened and a rosy-cheeked lad wearing a funny looking bell-boy hat stuck his head out onto the street.

"Are you Sebastian?" the young lad asked nicely.

I nodded my head and then he said, "Come along with me."

I was led down a dimly lit corridor by the young theatre worker, specks of dust floating onto old boxes and cane chests stacked high against the walls, the corridor disappearing further on, into a murky darkness. This was certainly not what I expected, totally different from the spectacular foyer that must be less than fifty yards away.

I followed the young lad past doors on our right, labelled in brass lettering: FOYER, STALLS, DRESS CIRCLES, BOXES. Then, no doors for quite a while.

Finally up ahead, I could see a small shaft of light coming out from a barely open double door, still on our right. I stopped to have a look through the inch wide gap between the two doors into what seemed like a huge abandoned ballroom, amazed to see a rotund red-faced man dancing in front of a similarly round and red-faced boy of perhaps six or seven years of age.

He was cutting a pretty good rug this big man, spinning his body in full turns and then stretching his arms forward and then back, up and then down while wiggling his fingers. The young fella must have liked the show because he clapped wildly at the large man, when he had finished.

The theatre lad poked me in the shoulder, urging me to move along. After twenty yards, he stopped and whispered.

"That's the boss and his son in there. He doesn't come in that often, but when he does, he hates people hanging around down here. He would flip his lid if he saw us ... and he really hates being watched, too."

A little further on, he pointed to a staircase on our right which led, almost straight up, into obscurity.

"Head to the top. There's a door on the right. Knock only once, not loudly, and then wait."

"Thanks," I said, although the young lad had already scooted halfway back down the corridor, before I finished the word.

After I had climbed about thirty steps, I could hear two voices and then giggling, coming from the darkness above.

Don't tell me this bloke has a girl up there? He hadn't mentioned anything about Elaine coming to the pictures, but who knows what this character would do.

I knocked gently on a small door that I could just make out in the pitch blackness at the top of the stairs and then waited, like I was told. I could hear fits of laughter coming from inside the room. After about thirty seconds the door opened towards me. William was standing there, a finger across his lips, chuckling like a big girl. This took me quite by surprise to see him like this, after what I'd recently seen at the City Baths.

"Come in, Seb," William whispered "This is the projection room of the Regent Theatre. Come and meet Sidney."

There was a large, shiny machine on the left-hand side of the room making a steady whirring sound, silver disks above and below at the front, a man toiling on the far side. I tried to take in my surroundings as fast as I could. This was a most unusual, stuffy and tight place to be in.

A large, round-faced bald man popped up from behind the machine.

"Sidney, meet Seb. He's a good friend of mine."

This William bloke has got more crap in him than a night cart.

I leant over to shake Sidney's hand.

"Pleased to meet you, Seb. William has talked about you. He says you're a good fighter, is that correct?" the large man asked in an accent I didn't recognise.

I gave an annoyed look at William.

"I think he's talking about the wrong man, Sidney," I replied, still embarrassed about my fight at the university. "I try to avoid fights if I can."

"Seb, Sidney's from Poland. He's only been here for four years. He is one of the hardest working people in the Aid for Spain movement, when he can. Unfortunately, he finds it hard to get away from the projector. There are only a couple of people in Australia that know how to work this monster of a machine."

"Nice to meet you, Sidney. I've never met anyone from Poland before ... actually, I'm not really sure where it is?"

"It's stuck between Germany and Russia, Seb. That's the problem." The large Polish man laughed out loud, his whole body quivering.

"Wait until you see this week's newsreels, Seb," William said excitedly. "There's a kangaroo called Peter in boxing gloves fighting some bloke. It's the funniest thing you'll ever see. Sidney showed it to me just before you got up here. There are plenty of other newsreels from around the world, I can show you them in Sidney's small reel viewer, if that's okay, Sid?"

"I don't mind Bill, but I do have to thread the film, 'reel' soon; the show as they say, must go on." Sidney grinned broadly and then disappeared behind the projector again.

I looked through the rectangular viewing portholes in the wall of the projection room, into the vast theatre. I could see several couples in their finest, searching up and down the aisles trying to locate their seats, only a couple of kids to be seen up here in the dress circle.

"Sit over here, Seb. Sidney has made up some rough seats for us to see the show. I wouldn't mind seeing the start of *Cain and Mabel*, if that's all right before we watch anything else. What d'ya say, Seb?"

He's laying it on a bit thick. I didn't even know who he was, an hour and a half ago.

"Yeah, that would be swell."

At least at the moment, he wasn't acting like the angry young man from the Aid for Spain stand in Emerald Hill, or a handler of two enormous bodyguards like he was at the Red Square, and nothing like the uppity senior he was outside the university. He does genuinely seem a different person up here, out of sight. Maybe, he should stop trying to impress everyone with his 'loose cannon' act.

But, I wasn't his friend, and I didn't like pretending I

was. He had to be up to something. What other explanation could there be for someone who knows what's happening on every street corner, wanting to be friends with a fellmonger.

I was really enjoying the performance of Marion Davies in *Cain and Mabel*; such a feisty character. Out of all the Hollywood stars, she's probably the closest to the down to earth country girls I'm used to. Clark Gable is a good actor too, but not in this flick — not at all convincing as a boxer, doesn't look like he could knock the skin off a rice pudding — and doubly ridiculous in a star-shaped boxing get-up.

At intermission, Sidney asked us if we would go down and get him a bottle of creaming soda to have with the cold meat and smelly cheese he laid out on small plates near his machine. William and I snuck back down the dusty corridor again, past the ballroom where the big man had danced for his son, which was dark and empty now. We turned left through the door marked 'Foyer', hearing the murmur of the patrons grow louder and louder, until suddenly, we were amongst them, almost blinded by the dazzling lights around the mezzanine.

"Wait here, Seb. I'll be back in a minute."

William wandered into, and then was lost in, the moving mass of chattering people.

It seemed I had to be prepared for anything, anytime with this bloke, and there was no way to tell how any of it would turn out. His unpredictability would make anyone nervous, but as far as today was concerned, I was starting to enjoy myself.

Five minutes later, I saw William push back through the crowd, holding three bottles of creaming soda high in his right hand, and what looked like a couple of really long pieces of liquorice in the other. Two girls followed behind. He really did look like the cat that got the cream, a huge grin on his face, when the two girls squeezed ahead of him.

"Seb, may I introduce you to Margaret and Danielle, they are Elaine and my best friends at the university. Truthfully, they should be preparing for tutorials but can't resist Clark Gable at all," William said, showing off.

"Pleased to meet you, Seb" Margaret nodded, followed by Danielle, before shaking my hand in turn.

"I believe your sister is working with Madeline in our kitchen today. Has she cooked before, Seb?" Margaret asked, though fairly sure of the answer.

"Yes, she loves cooking more than anything," I replied. "Very nice to meet you both," I said and then, unsure of what to say next, looked to William to fill the silence.

"Seb's sister, whose name, I am sad to say, I have momentarily forgotten, has just arrived down from the Wimmera. I think with her love of cooking, and with Madeline being so nice, the union of the two should work out mutually beneficial."

Lucky, you don't know what Madeline thinks of you.

"Her name is Leticia, but she prefers Lettie," I said, looking at the smarmy reaction on William's face, knowing that he would worm Lettie's name out of me, somehow. "So, fingers crossed she has a good day."

William's two friends from the university were both pretty; smart and pretty, a good combination. Danielle was the prettiest to me, with pitch black wavy hair and a great smile — and miles out of my league.

"We'd better get back to Sidney, Seb. He's doesn't have much time to eat during intermission. So, I will say *adieu* girls, and see you back in the Common Room in due course."

"Nice meeting you, Danielle, Margaret, and don't be afraid to say hello to Lettie in the kitchen. If she gets the position, that is."

I had shaken both their hands again before we left. Danielle's hand seemed to hold on longer than Margaret's, and she also turned around to give me a tiny smile, before heading up the stairs that led back into the theatre stalls.

William handed me a soda and a liquorice strap and then gave me a small pat on the shoulder, indicating that I should head back towards the corridor.

"How much do I owe ya, William?" I asked, moving slowly away from the crowd, "I like to pay my own way."

"Then, pay me nothing, Seb. That's what I paid. A lot of people appreciate what we're doing."

"We!" I shot back. "I haven't done anything. I'm not part

of your cause. I have a family that needs me more than people on the other side of the world that I don't know."

"Yes, 'we', Sebastian. I think you want to be more than a fellmonger at Cooks. You want a say in your life. I've seen it before," William proclaimed, as we walked through the 'Staff Only' door and then turned right into the dimly lit corridor, before speaking to the emptiness in front of him as he strode along.

"My father would have given up his trade as a mason, if he had to, when he arrived in Adelaide on a ship from Germany, shortly before the Great War. Fortunately, for my father, the demand for masons at the time could never be met." William's stride increased, along with his enthusiasm for the subject.

"Although, financially secure, he soon became dissatisfied working for his mostly 'Anglophile' bosses, who took every opportunity to remind him that he was the hated enemy. When he bought a rundown concrete works for a song, the good citizens of Adelaide laughed at him, until he began employing their sons. He gave them a fair day's pay, for a fair day's work. Now, they respect him, and so do I."

William stopped at the bottom of the stairs that led up to the projection room.

"I worked in the concrete works at every opportunity, outside of school. I liked the honesty of the men in the crushing mill, and would have happily worked there longer, but my father told me 'Knowledge, always wins out over brute strength'. So, I was sent to Melbourne University, and told not to come back until I was my own man."

We were both silent for a second, unsure if there was anything more we needed to say to each other.

I'd never had to question myself before. Why would I, my life was simple? I would be working in the job Aunty May teed up for me, for the foreseeable future and probably beyond. But, I had a gnawing feeling that I should make a stand for myself while I still had time, and not just accept the cards as they were dealt.

"If you want to go, Sebastian, that's fine by me. You're not a prisoner," William asserted. "Now, I must get back to Sidney."

William turned his back on me and then started his steep walk up the stairs. I immediately felt that perhaps I'd been unfair to this bloke. He was different, that was for sure, but maybe he did care about people a lot more than I first thought. Why hadn't I given him the same fair go as I gave everyone else?

"Are there any more newsreels that have Peter the Kangaroo in them?" I yelled out to William, who stopped midway up the stairs. "I'd like to see 'em if there are."

After a few seconds, he turned around and said, "Yeah, Sidney has one that was filmed at Melbourne Zoo, only a couple of months ago, where he rips a hessian bag apart.

It's hilarious. Do ya wanna go up and see if we can find it?"

I headed up the stairs behind William, feeling a sense of relief that I'd made the right decision to stay.

*

The odour of Sidney's stinky orange cheese had filled the small projection room. I had to politely refuse Sidney's offer to try some, but, William had no qualms about scoffing down a large slice, saying that to appreciate life one had to try new things, as if I'd been brought up in a cave.

William searched the side of a stack of film cans that were leaning against the far wall of the projection room. Sidney left us to it, getting back to the second half of *Cain and Mabel*, which I quietly would have liked to as well, but resigned myself to seeing what gems William came up with.

William pulled out five film cans and then set them down next to the reel viewer, holding one up, with a big grin on his face.

"I've got it. Peter the Kangaroo in Melbourne!"

We took it in turns to look down the viewer at the short silent film. It was a real crack-up, Peter ripped a hessian bag filled with wool into a thousand pieces, bits flying in all directions. It shouldn't have been funny, but it was. Then, we watched a British Pathé newsreel on the Italian

Army in Abyssinia, which was rolling artillery, trucks and tanks, up and down rough dusty roads, in pursuit of a native army that appeared to have only spears and ancient rifles. A bit embarrassing I thought for the Italians, taking on an enemy, they couldn't help but beat.

On one reel, a lady called Nola Reid danced a daring version of the can-can. On another, the Mitchell's Christian Singers and Bing Crosby sang 'I'm An Old Cowhand'. There was too much war footage on the next reel for my liking, so I suggested to William that we get back to watching *Cain and Mabel*.

"There's a new reel on the floor, next to the stack, Bill," Sidney called to us. "It's just come in from London, I'm told there's lots about Spain in it. The boys from the Keno want me to clean it up for the Aid committee's lantern shows. I haven't seen it yet, but it's less than three weeks old. See what you think."

I only had to watch thirty seconds of *Defenders of Madrid* to realise that it would be too much for most people to watch. The poor buggers in Madrid were going off to work while bombs fell all around them. It was courageous and insane at the same time. I stopped watching, but William wouldn't leave the viewer.

All of a sudden, he got up and punched the metal back wall of the projection room, setting off a loud vibrating sound that must have been heard from outside our tiny confines.

Sidney shot up, surprised and annoyed by the sound that William had made, *Cain and Mabel* still flickering in the background.

"Sidney, I'm so sorry!" William apologised immediately. "I don't want to think about Spain any more."

William, obviously very upset by what he'd seen, said sorry to me as well and then headed out the door and could be heard racing down the precarious stairs.

Sidney put up his hand to stop me following him; his expression seemed to indicate that he knew what was wrong.

"I can't tell you why he gets so angry, but he has a very good reason, I can assure you of that. I'm sure he will tell you when the time is right. Stay and watch the end of the film, he will be fine."

*

I had hit a wall myself before the movie finished. My eyes barely staying open long enough to find out what happened to Clark and Marion. This day, that had kept getting bigger and bigger, was finally catching up to me.

When the film ended, Sidney told me jokingly that he had to kick me out now. He had to watch a newsreel that he should have watched earlier, before letting William watch it. Sidney repeated, not to worry about William. "He's always been a bit up and down," he said. I thought there might have been a pattern.

I thanked Sidney for allowing me into his workplace to watch the latest newsreels and a great film. Sidney said I was welcome back anytime, and to bring a friend if I liked. All I had to do was say to the staff in the confection-ery stand in the foyer that I wanted to see Sidney.

I could still hear Sidney laughing to himself, when I was halfway down the steep stairs that led from his projection room.

I exited the 'Stage Door,' knowing I had to get back to Aunty May's fairly soon. I badly needed a kip or else I wouldn't make it through dinner and then out again to pick up Lettie later in the evening. I wondered whether I should go back towards the university to see if William was somewhere along the way, but honestly, the short time I'd had with him was enough for the moment. I just wanted Lettie to get the job with Madeline in the college kitchen; that was all I wanted to think about for the time being.

I started to shiver and felt a chill seep into my bones, well before I attempted to cross over a very busy Victo-ria Street, to make my way up to Lygon. I was looking forward to hitting the sack hard.

On a bench outside Trades Hall, my attention was drawn to the now distinctive green and white jacket of a King's College senior. It was William, sitting alone, look-ing rather sheepish.

"Hi, Seb. Did you enjoy the movie?" he asked. "Elaine

enjoyed it last week, during a break between tutorials." William stood up, looking grateful I had come along.

"Thanks. It was great. The whole lot. What an interesting bloke Sidney is, and he's got the best job in the world. Ya'd never get bored in that caper. Always something to see," I said cheerily, trying to lighten up the mood.

"My pleasure, Seb."

William went quiet and looked down at the ground. I knew he had something he wanted to say but, for a change, seemed a little lost.

"My Dad sent me to Melbourne and the university, so that I would make my own way in life, not to follow his. But, all I wanted to do was be like him ... don't get me wrong, Sebastian. I love Elaine and our friends at the university; they keep me focused. You may not understand it, but to me, the whole world order is being torn down. I can see it clearly. I'm the editor of *The Proletarian*, a university newspaper. I try to make people aware of the change that is coming, but it's not enough. What is needed is action, and the action is overseas," William said turning to look to the north-west.

"It's so frustrating, acting out the silly anachronistic traditions of the King's College, when I know their world will soon be gone."

I may not understand much but I knew when someone was being a spoilt brat and not appreciating the wonderful opportunity laid at their feet. A chance that kept him out of the grinding poverty so many people have to live with.

My Dad burnt down his truck, to try and give Robbie a chance at university.

"Sidney said there was a good reason why you got angry. I don't think that sounds like a good reason to me, not liking the hundreds of opportunities a university education can give you. It was ready for the taking ... for you, and not many others," I said curtly, frustrated with his demeaning attitude.

William started to move from side to side, his teeth clenching together.

"Don't be naïve, Seb. You don't know what's happening, it's too personal. I have to deal with it myself."

"My Dad says it's always best to talk things through. I don't know a lot about anything, but for me that sounds good advice. So, if you don't tell me what's goin' on, I'm leavin', right now!" I threatened as seriously as I could muster, before feigning to move away. "Sorry, but I have people other than myself to think of."

I waited a little longer, to see if William would make an effort to explain his selfishness.

"Righto, I'm goin'," I said again, tired of his supposed problems. "I haven't got time to wait around. I have a sister to think of."

"Elaine's sister Aggy is in Spain at the moment."

I looked at William, unsure of what sort of response he

wanted, but also knowing that it can't be a good place to be at this moment.

"What is she doing there?" I asked, genuinely, "Is she a nurse?"

"When she has to. The last time we heard from her, she was working as an interpreter with a British medical unit not far from the Aragon front. She trained as a field orderly with the Red Cross a year ago in Rome, hoping to go to Eritrea, but was barred from boarding the only ship from Italy to the main port of Massawa. So, she went to stay with her family, who were writing and holiday-ing near Barcelona. Then, the workers' uprising began in Catalonia. When Elaine and her family, the Parmenters, felt they should leave, Aggy insisted on staying behind."

"Elaine and her family must be terribly worried about her. Although, where she is at the moment, may be a long way from the fighting," I said trying my hardest to say the right thing.

"Elaine is worried sick though no-one would ever notice. She keeps it so well hidden. But, I know how much it hurts her."

William ran his hands through his hair and then rubbed his forehead, his eyes closed.

"But, that's not the worst of it," he mumbled to himself.

"There is a rumour coming out of Spain, which is not uncommon in itself, except I have heard it again and again from comrades I know that have excellent sources in the Socialist Party in Spain. They say an Australian woman working near the Aragon front, is under suspicion of being a spy for the Nationalists. Communications are difficult with Spain, of course, but I believe there are only four Australian women on that front."

"And, I haven't told Elaine or her family yet," William said even quieter, shaking his head, before he sat back down, leaning hard against the bench.

"Now, I'm at a loss to know what to do, Sebastian," William said looking to the sky.

I imagined William was only trying to protect Elaine's family, until he had the facts. But the Parmenters, after living there, must have been well aware of the dangers Aggy would face in Spain. William needed to tell them, because nothing is surer, this big secret would only come back to bite him hard on the backside, further down the track.

"I'm in regular contact with my comrades, and I hope to see two of them this evening. I know what I need to do now, so don't be concerned, Seb. I will make sure no-one gets hurt by this."

William had dismissed me offhand, which was fine. He was perhaps relieved to be able to unload some of his worries onto someone not personally involved with his dilemma.

After a few minutes William composed himself, taking on the stiff upper-lip bearing of a college senior again, from the same anachronistic world he had demeaned only minutes earlier.

"Were Elaine and her family born in Britain, William? They seem quite familiar with Europe. I hope I'm not snooping, but that seems to me where their interests lie," I asked, not having heard of a family like Elaine's before.

This question grabbed William's attention, his eyes lighting up as I sat down beside him.

"No, Elaine's mother, Enid, was born near the Heathcote goldfields. She loves the country, more than anything. Apparently, she had to be dragged kicking and screaming to board at the King's College, when she was eighteen."

"That's my Mum's name, Enid," I threw in. William then gave me the slightest sign of acknowledgement, before continuing.

"Elaine's father, Blake, was born on a cattle station in Northern Queensland. He was on horseback alongside Aboriginal jackeroos by the age of eight and able to speak their language by eleven. Blake was eventually sent to a boarding school in Brisbane, where he excelled in Literature, moving down to Melbourne University a few years later to complete his literary degree."

"He met Elaine's mother in the campus library, while fighting over a Joseph Furphy book they both wished to take out. From there, they fell into the same circles and, of course, in love. After graduating, they travelled to London to work in the large publishing houses that control the Australian book market. After several years in Europe, they returned to tour the length and breadth of Australia. They are amazing people, Seb," William said, speaking with pride, before standing up with a renewed enthusiasm.

"They have lost count of the number of books and articles they have written, but most of all, they have never lost faith in Australian literature. Elaine says she owes her confidence in the future to her parents.

"On witnessing the joy of the Catalonian people finally breaking free of centuries of oppression, they couldn't stand by and let the same privileged classes of the church, and the landowners return to make them suffer again, so they decided to help form the Spanish Aid Committee. Enid is president, but they both work tirelessly for the cause. I might sound a little sycophantic, but if you ever get the chance to meet them, you will feel the same way."

"They sound great, William. It's such a rare thing to see people give up so much of their lives for others," I wasn't really sure what I was saying, but William kept nodding his head anyway.

"Elaine and her family have been working so hard for many, many months for the Spanish cause that they have decided to rest for a few days, before recommencing their efforts. They deserve a break, which is part of the reason ..." William looked away briefly, before continuing.

"After the official end of Spanish Month, on Sunday they are holding a soirée at their home in Camberwell, to let their hair down, if only for a short time."

"If anyone deserves a break it sounds like they do, William, and probably more than a couple of days."

"That they do."

I knew from that short response, it was time we went our separate ways. If, Lettie gets the job in the kitchen, there's a good chance I will run into William again, although I wouldn't necessarily go looking for him.

"Thanks again for the flicks, William, and sorry for the 'know-all' remark," I said as I got up, before putting out my hand for William to shake, which he did firmly. "And, don't be afraid to say hello to Lettie in the kitchen. I think it would be good if you met. But, that's up to you."

"I have a busy week organising a debate with our nemesis, the Campeins, but I will find time to introduce myself to Lettie. That is a promise."

"Are you going up Lygon Street?" I asked half-heartedly. "You could cut across Argyle Square."

"No, while I'm at Trades Hall I'll drop in on some chaps I know. They might have some more news from Spain."

I gave a small nod to William and then turned to walk up Lygon Street, feeling too wide awake now for a kip.

*

Lettie appeared out of the shadows of the main college hall, which was lit up now like a palace against the pitch black sky. As Lettie walked towards me and joined the wide, curved driveway, she was flanked by the same tall senior I had a run in with last Sunday. They seemed to be hitting it off quite well, which made me think that perhaps I'd been a little too hard on college seniors of late.

The tall senior left Lettie to finish the final few yards to the college gate, the biggest smile breaking out on her face as she came up to me.

"Thank you! Thank you! Thank you!" was all Lettie said, before she gave me a huge hug.

I think she liked the job.

"Madeline is wonderful, she has so much knowledge about how to prepare food, she pushes everyone so hard to get it out on time; she has to!" Lettie exclaimed without taking a breath. "I was told to come back Monday morning, and if I don't muck up in a fortnight, I've got a job. Wooee!"

Lettie was over the moon, but I could also see she was exhausted.

I would make her a cup of tea in the morning and then tell her about my incredible day out, with a most unusual college senior.

8

The Quadrangle Garden

"I bet that's ya sister, young Seb," Lenny squawked out, loud enough for all the workers nearby to hear, before opening the factory gate to give us our freedom for another day.

I looked across the small lane that Cooks was set on, to see Lettie standing on the footpath opposite, dressed in the new pink uniform that Madeline supplied her with on the first day of her trial. At first glance Lettie looked happy enough, but what would make her come so far out of her way?

The first thing that sprang to mind was that things hadn't worked out for Lettie in the kitchen, and Madeline had to let her go. She would be devastated if that was the case. The only other thought was that it had something to do with home, but Lettie wouldn't have had near enough time to get back to Aunty May's, hear any news and then work her way back to North Melbourne, before I knocked off.

But, whatever it was, it had to be damn important.

As soon as Lettie saw me, she gave me a small wave and a smile, which eased my mind a lot. We had hardly spoken since Sunday morning, when I told her about my trip into the city with William. Only the day before we had both agreed he must be some sort of madman, so why, she complained, had I lost any sense of reason and gone off with him? Lettie had me cold with that.

Sunday afternoon, Lettie kept going on and on about why I had forgotten about our plan to go to the pictures together that day, saying she would have loved to have seen *Cain and Mabel*, as her first outing in the city for years. I told her that we could still go and see the movie, and as many movies as we liked, all we had to do was visit Sidney at the Regent Theatre, but she said that didn't sound like the right thing to do.

Nothing was going to make Lettie happy on Sunday, so I left her on her own and went out for a long walk. When I came back a couple of hours later, Aunty May told me Lettie had taken herself off to her room, not long after I'd left. When she checked on her shortly afterwards, Lettie was fast asleep.

"Hello, Lettie. What brings you down to Hotham Hill on this fine Tuesday afternoon?" the foreman yelled out across the lane.

"Hi, Mr Simonds. It was such a beautiful day, I thought I'd go for a stroll and see if Seb wanted some company on his way home," Lettie replied, giving my foreman a wave as he headed off, "We'll see you back home for dinner, then."

Lettie was getting on far too well with Aunty May's beloved Barry for my liking.

Strangely, I hadn't known what the foreman's full name was, up until then, and to be fair, the foreman and the leading hand hadn't been too bad during the week. Maybe, they had hearts after all.

"That's Seb's sister, Lettie," Lenny jabbered to the stragglers, as they exited the corrugated iron factory gate, before slamming it shut behind them.

A couple of trucks were facing off in our cramped laneway, neither driver willing to give an inch to his opposite, and preventing me from reaching the other side of the lane to find out what really brought Lettie here.

When I finally made a dash for it behind the closest truck and reached the footpath on the other side, Lettie appeared surprisingly calm and relaxed.

"Everything 'right, Lett? Did something happen in the kitchen?"

"No, Grub. Everything's fine," Lettie replied, with a funny smirk on her face. "Fine and dandy."

Then, Lettie seemed to shiver with nerves, which only made me more confused.

"We've been invited to a soirée in Camberwell, Grub," Lettie blurted out. "What d'ya think of that?"

"Who told ya that, Lett, who invited us? Was it the senior, or his girlfriend Elaine? It has to be one of them two."

"Let's go, Grub. I'll tell ya about it on the way home. It's a doozy!"

*

A bright sun and warm breeze on our backs made the rundown backstreets of North Melbourne seem a whole lot cheerier for Lettie and me. We wound our way back towards home, beside grimy-faced workers who had just exited the factories and warehouses that were the only reason anyone ventured into these parts.

I could see Lettie's mind ticking over and over, making sure she got the story right before she would let me hear any more of it. It must be one hell of a story.

"Grub, remember you said you met two girls at the Regent? Friends of your new college mate?" Lettie asked while not missing a beat over the cracked and uneven footpath.

"He's not a mate, Lett, probably won't run into him again 'cept by accident 'round Carlton, or at the college. The girls were Danielle and Margaret, I think," I replied, knowing full well who they were.

"That's them. They came to the delivery door this morning, asking Madeline if they could talk to me for a minute. Madeline told me not to leave her one short for too long. The girls said you told them it would be nice if they came to say hello to me. Why did ya have to say that for Grub, I felt so embarrassed?"

Shoot! I forgot to tell Lettie that William had promised to visit her as well.

"Honestly, Lett. I didn't think they were serious, I promise," I said looking to quickly worm my way out of this. "Did they say anything about me?"

"Sometimes Grub, I wonder if you're twenty."

A minute later, as we straightened for the long haul down Queensberry Street into Carlton, Lettie suddenly stopped, pulling two ribbons out of her flour-covered coat pocket, lifting them up to show me.

"Look what they gave me, Grub. Margaret gave me the green one, Danielle the white one," she said placing them next to her tightly curled auburn hair.

"Do ya like 'em, Grub?"

I nodded my approval, thinking it wouldn't be such a bad thing if Lettie got to know the girls.

"They told me the colours were very special to them. Green and white are the colours of the University Peace Group, which they're both passionate about, as well as that of the college, of course. It's very thoughtful of them, don't you think?"

"Yeah, they seemed nice at the theatre, Lett. They must be sure ya stayin' on."

"I dunno, Grub. Madeline never gives away a thing, either way, but what happened during my break after lunch service was funny though. The girls told me that the Peace Group was having an afternoon meeting in the Quadrangle Garden and anyone was allowed to come along and join in, so I told 'em I would try to make it if I finished my clean-up on time."

"It took me yonks to find them in the campus. It was right in the middle of a beautiful building with arched verandahs, not really a garden in the quadrangle, just a few camellias. There were lots of people though, it surprised me. Margaret and Danielle were standing proudly in front of everyone, holding up a banner with 'World Peace' on it, green and white ribbons in their hair. A tall, solid bloke, maybe a minister was doin' all the talkin'. He said that Spain was behind Great Britain, because the Catholic Church ran all the schools in Spain. Is that right, Grub?"

"Wouldn't have a clue, Lett. The Catholic Church runs a lot of schools here, they seem all right to me."

"A lot of people were trying to drown out this big man by jeering and laughing, and they said some pretty nasty things to him. The meeting was starting to get a bit out of hand and I was worried that Margaret and Danielle might get caught up in the middle of a fight. Then suddenly, a well-dressed man stood up and stepped very close to the speaker, pointing a finger between his eyes, yelling loudly 'You are a liar, a damn liar ... and a bloody turncoat too!' to the roar of one section of the crowd."

"I don't know what he meant by that Grub, but Margaret stepped forward, yelling loudly herself for everybody to be quiet. She told the well-dressed man that he had 'over-stepped the mark with his comments, and he should leave the meeting, NOW!' It was a brave thing for Margaret to do with the unsettled crowd and this man staring at her in a kind of daze, not like he was drunk, but something else. That man then urged his supporters in the crowd to follow him from the quadrangle, which they did, to the loud booing from the crowd left behind. The people who walked out were mostly dressed in black gowns with a white cross and maybe Catholic symbols on 'em."

"Madeline did say something the other day about things getting a little out of hand on campus, Lett. It might be best to stay away from those meetings."

"Stop fussin' Grub, nothin' happened."

I was enjoying my walk back home from work with Lettie, especially the last stretch we were on now, through the quiet back lanes near Aunty May's. The weeping willows and peppercorn trees whipping overhead made us feel like we were almost back home in the country again.

I knew there had to be more to Lettie's story than a fiery meeting at the university, so I gently urged her to get to the point.

"If the girls didn't invite us, who did, Lett?"

Lettie stopped to give herself a quick dust down before we took on the last couple of hundred yards to Aunty May's.

"Before I got back to the kitchen, at the big bike sheds near the oval, a King's College girl came running up to me from behind, calling out for me to stop. She startled me a bit, my mind was miles away in the kitchen. She asked if I could spare a minute, so she could apologise about a misunderstanding that had happened. I told her I had to get back to the kitchen pretty soon, but she could walk with me if she liked."

"She said her name was Elaine and that she had met you at the Aid for Spain stand in Emerald Hill and liked that you had shown so much interest in their cause, even after your new mate William had been very rude to you. She said it was her fault how things became so confused, although she said William's erratic behaviour of late hadn't helped. After we had talked for a while, I was surprised how much we had in common. She seems really nice, Grub."

"Yeah, she was very friendly when I met her in Emerald Hill. And quite persuasive."

"Elaine said the confusion came about when a senior came racing into the Junior Common Room on Sunday before last while she was studying with William. He was looking for a tutor or a professor to come with him to have a look at a rough looking bloke who had been found wandering in the grounds. The senior said that the intruder pretended to be looking for work for his sister."

"Elaine said William's eyes lit up when the senior

said that the young man had a cut under his chin. Then William went with the senior to have a look for himself, but didn't return for over an hour."

Lettie and I stopped in the lane, a few yards back from Aunty May's, not wanting this story to make it inside.

"So, William must have followed me home, the sneaky bugger," I said sarcastically as some of the pieces to this puzzle started falling into place.

"No wonder he knows so much about me. He probably spoke to old Reg, he's always hangin' around out the front wanting a chin wag."

And Reg can never remember Lettie's name

"Elaine said she was so angry with William for spying on you, but he reckoned he only did it because he had run into you four times in a fortnight, and didn't like that sort of coincidence."

"Yeah, it would look a bit suspicious, but why didn't he just stop and ask me," I wondered shaking my head.

"Elaine said he wanted to know exactly who you were before introducing himself properly. William told Elaine that he would make amends somehow, so he went to see Madeline to convince her that the young man who attempted to visit her was only looking out for his sister and that she should consider helping her with work, if the opportunity arose.

"Elaine said that at no time were William or her trying to make me feel unwelcome in the college.

"I told Elaine that perhaps her boyfriend might be a little too crazed to be a college senior, which she understood in part, but also said I couldn't know the William she does."

"Elaine confided in me that she wished for just one day, not only William but her whole family lived a normal life, and weren't so passionate about making the world a better place for other people, and concentrated on looking after the ones that were closest to them. Then, she wouldn't have to worry so much.

"I felt a bit awkward that she was telling me this, Grub. Not knowing her. Did William say anything on Saturday about Elaine's family?"

"No, he did say that I would be most impressed if I ever met them, though," I replied, keeping it short and sweet. I didn't want Lettie to know about Elaine's sister being in trouble in Spain, she had enough to deal with without that.

"I said to Elaine that we should perhaps put all this mix-up behind us, and act as if it never happened, and maybe one day we could go out as a group for a picnic, or to a coffee palace. Elaine thought that would be a nice change. After all, you and William had a day in the city."

"That wasn't my idea, Lett," I chipped in.

"Before I went back into the kitchen, I asked Elaine if the senior standing under a nearby oak tree looking rather nervous was William, and if so, could she please bring him around to the kitchen after dinner so I could finally meet this bloke you're always goin' on about.

"When they came around to the kitchen door after service, I was surprised how charming William was, and he's not at all bad looking either, Grub," Lettie said stripping small cream flowers off the peppercorn tree just above her head.

That was a big turnaround from Sunday.

"Elaine said there was a lot happening at the uni, and with the Aid committee at the moment, so the only opportunity, if we were free on Sunday evening, would be to go with them to a soirée at her parent's house in Camberwell. She would have to phone first, but she was sure it would be fine."

"I remember on Saturday, William talking about a soirée or some such at Elaine's parents, but I didn't imagine we would get invited to it," I said leaning hard against the paling fence.

"I told Elaine we'd both be delighted to go to the soirée with them," Lettie giggled as she smiled, her head leant to the side. "I hope ya don't mind, Grub."

"They're different to us, Lett," I replied, taking a deep breath.

9

Soirée

On Thursday the reality of what we'd accepted dawned upon us. We had until Sunday afternoon to work out what people wear to soirées. We wondered what made a soirée different to any other do and were we just kidding ourselves to think we could fit into William and Elaine's circle? Lettie was quiet on Thursday, like me; we were not sure what we'd let ourselves in for. It wouldn't have taken much for either of us to pull out.

We told Aunty May on Thursday night about the soirée; we had to, there was no way we could get around it. We couldn't tell her on Sunday that we had our glad rags on to go to church — she knows we never go. Aunty May said the Parmenters were quite a 'radical family' for Melbourne, no-one was sure if they were communists or not. Although, she hinted that most of their friends could be called 'fellow travellers', but at least they were 'prominent Australians'.

Aunty May said she had read one of Blake Parmenter's books years ago called *Men Are Human, Too!*, and loved it. She couldn't give her approval for us to go, but she would help us if we needed to know what went on at a soirée, after all she had gone to several in the Cape Colony thirty-odd years ago.

When I asked Aunty May if I would need a suit and tie for the do, she said that a white dinner jacket with a bow-tie was *de rigueur* for a soirée on the *veldt*. Aunty May said that Heinrich in his rush to leave years ago had left behind some of his clothes, and she would be happy if I went through them to pick out something to wear, but she wouldn't help. Lettie gave me an elbow in the side, whispering for me not to ask on her behalf, saying later on that she couldn't have stood Aunty May trying to fit her into one of her old dress designs that had no shape at all.

Lettie confided in Madeline on Friday that she was going to a soirée at the Parmenter's house on Sunday, and didn't have a clue what to wear, or how to act around people who were so well known. Lettie said she could see the surprise on Madeline's face when she mentioned the Parmenters, but said she could borrow some of her clothes, if Lettie would do her a big favour Saturday lunchtime; pick up Bernadette from a birthday party at the Children's Hospital that was finishing at an awkward time for the kitchen. Lettie told Madeline she had been waiting for an opportunity to see Bernadette again and jumped at the chance.

On Saturday, Madeline asked Lettie to leave the

kitchen half an hour earlier than expected to pick up Bernadette, just in case the party finished ahead of time. As Lettie wandered through the wards, she said she couldn't help but cry; so many children locked in horrible metal machines, or struggling to walk in callipers, others being pushed around in wheelchairs. She said the smiles on the faces of the children defied all logic considering what they had to bear each day. Lettie spoke to a few of the volunteers and nurses in the ward before wheeling Bernadette home, one volunteer said the hospital was turning away thirty children a day at the moment, sending most to temporary facilities in the southern suburbs.

At Madeline's house the mood turned a lot brighter, with mother and daughter making a fuss over Lettie. Bernadette made herself judge of every dress that Lettie tried on, dismissing anything too dull. They all agreed on one dress; the one which Madeline said was her 'standard', and didn't want back unless it was in exactly the same condition as it left.

Lettie and I had a bit of a scare ourselves on Sunday morning, with the whole Carlton neighbourhood covered in a thick, rolling fog which appeared out of nowhere and looked like it wanted to stay. According to *The Argus*, Sunday would be fine and sunny with a light westerly breeze.

Not that it would make much of a difference to my get-up for the soirée; a musty green jacket with grey pinstripes, a white round-collared shirt and a black tie was fashionable in any season. Aunty May suggested a bow-tie would be more suitable for the round collar, but I said bow-ties were only for people with tickets on themselves.

*

"Stop pinching your cheeks!" I yelled at Lettie, pretending to be angry "They're already red raw."

Lettie had been poking and pulling at her face, hair, dress and everything else, since we arrived twenty minutes earlier than necessary outside St Pauls Cathedral, where she had arranged for us to meet Elaine and William to catch a tram to Camberwell.

"Shush, Grub," Lettie grumbled while waving me away and then, turned around to look for anything that resembled a mirror. The only thing Lettie could find remotely fitting the bill was the glassed-in cabinet that housed today's ecclesiastic program for the massive cathedral. The small amount of reflection in the glass kept Lettie busy enough to spare the Flinders Street footpath any more wear and tear.

Lettie kept pulling down on the aqua-blue frock she borrowed from Madeline, as she peered into the cabinet, saying that it was a smidge tight for her, but loved the colour too much not to wear it.

Lettie had woven the green and white ribbons that

Margaret and Danielle had given her into a short ponytail, which didn't really go with the small white disc-shaped hat, Aunty May told her she had to wear. Lettie insisted she wouldn't wear the hat without the ribbons.

The sun had done the right thing by early afternoon, burning off the persistent fog, leaving behind a sunny but coolish day, making it a lot more comfortable to wear my heavy green dinner jacket.

"There they are!" Lettie yelled out, giving her hair, dress and ribbons another round of attention, in between waving to her two new friends.

Elaine and William both looked relaxed and confident as they strode towards us beside the cathedral lawn. Elaine in a long, bright yellow and white, vertically striped dress with a small white hat, William sporting a black dinner jacket with a plain white, pointy collared shirt, and no tie. I made up my mind right there and then, my tie would have to go, well before we reached the soirée.

"Don't they look great, Grub? They're so modern in the way they dress," said Lettie, in awe.

They did look swell, but that only made me think more about the huge gulf between us.

"We've finally made it," exclaimed Elaine, catching her breath, beaming a smile out to us. "How are you both doing, today?"

Elaine was a very pretty young woman, and the nicest person, but for some reason not my type.

"How are you, both?" William asked stepping forward to shake my hand.

"Great thanks, William," Lettie gushed. "We were a bit worried about the fog this morning, but look at it now, couldn't have turned out better for a soirée."

"I'm good, too," I replied and then, unnecessarily. "Now, are you sure it's fine, us going to your parents' house, Elaine?"

"Elaine called her parents. They are more than happy that you come along," William jumped in coolly, not really making Lettie or I feel that welcome. If I was on my own, I would have made up any old excuse to leave. If William was in one of his moods, I didn't want to be around him.

"Lettie, do you want to go over to the station? We can get something to eat for the trip. The boys will be right on their own, won't you boys?" Elaine asked, putting her hand around Lettie's arm, leading her towards the corner. I was stuck with a silent William, thinking that this day was about to turn sour any second.

"Last Saturday, before we went over the road to the Regent Theatre," I started to ask tentatively, "you were looking around for quite a long time along Swanston Street and then up and down Collins. What ..."

"It's none of your business," William snapped. "I can tell you're not interested. So leave it at that."

If anyone needs the shit beaten out of them, it's this bludger.

I'll try to get through the day for Lettie's sake, but after that, I'm finished with him.

"Ever since you told me about Elaine's sister in Spain, I haven't been able to stop worrying about Elaine, and how hard it must be for her, not knowing whether her sister was safe. If any one of my family was in danger like that ..." I stopped and then shook my head.

"When Lettie said that Elaine came up to her to apologise about my stupid mistake of wandering, uninvited into the college. I thought that we were the last people she should be worryin' about, and Lettie would agree ... if she knew ... so you can go to hell!"

William knew not to say anything back to me.

I wandered over to the cathedral. A few minutes later I saw Lettie and Elaine running madly across Swanston Street like they had been friends all their lives, a policeman holding up traffic, until they cleared the road.

I think I hid my disappointment at William's behaviour quite well from the girls after they returned from their foraging trip with a couple of paper bags each. Thankfully, Lettie didn't seem to notice anything, and I was doubly determined that William wasn't going to ruin our day. After all, it was Elaine who invited us, not him.

"We got some dried apricots and salted peanuts for the trip, Seb," Lettie explained, offering me some peanuts.

"We're gonna be thirsty by the time we get there," I added.

"Don't worry, Seb. Mr Parmenter makes his own home brew. I think it's the best ale I've ever tasted. I'll crack one open for us, as soon as we get there," William said enthusiastically, playing along with the game convincingly.

The new tram arrived a little earlier than expected, but perfectly on time for the four of us. We were toey to get our trip to Camberwell underway.

Once we had settled onto the wooden bench seats, Lettie and Elaine next to each other on the angle of two seats chatting away, William on the outside of Elaine facing forward, me looking straight ahead, watching the city disappear. I started to wonder what possibly could have happened in William's life, to make him turn into the angry young man he was now.

"Trams have only been running directly to Camberwell for about a year, Seb. Did you know that?" William threw in out of the blue. "Before that we had to get off the trolley tram at the Yarra and then get on a new tram to Elaine's place. It took a lot longer, didn't it, Lan?"

Elaine nodded, as Lettie jumped in.

"They should put cable-tram dummies out front of these trams, it would work a treat. It'd be a shame if they got rid of them completely, don't ya think?"

"In winter, it would be a bit fresh in the open air all the way to the city for us Camberwell girls, Lettie," chuckled Elaine, passing around the bag of dried apricots.

"All the cable-trams will be gone in a year," William

stated clinically. "I talked to a few gripmen the other day. They reckon their days were numbered."

We were starting to relax with each other, as we passed along a fairly quiet and still foggy Bridge Road in Richmond, before crossing the Yarra into a lot more affluent Hawthorn.

After about twenty minutes into our trip, I said to the others that I had to get off these wooden benches, and have a stretch, or else I wouldn't be able to move my sore right leg by the time we get to Camberwell.

"I'll come along with you, Seb. I'm getting a sore behind, myself," William joined in, jumping up and then following right behind me.

When we reached the front of the tram, well out of earshot of the girls, William came up close to me.

"I was looking for signs of trouble."

"What are you talking about?" I replied, failing to connect with his comment.

"Before we went to the Regent, I was looking out for our rivals at the university, those pretend Catholics; the Campeins. They've threatened to expose the Spanish Aid Committee as a front for the Communist Party. Which it isn't. The Commies give us money, and lots of it, that's all. We found out the Campeins were planning to ransack one of our stands in Collins Street, or our storage rooms, just up from the Regent."

"So, why did you drag me along, just to keep you

company while you play your silly games?" I asked bitterly, thinking all his talk about me being inspirational to him was crap.

William was silent for a second, looking at the other passengers and the conductor nearby.

"I need a friend who is not political, simple as that. So many people I know mirror their party's manifesto, it is so tedious. I need honesty, so I don't become anyone's fool," William whispered.

This bloke doesn't know who he is. I feel sorry for him more than anything.

"Did anything happen with the Campeins, did they ransack a stand?" I asked, expecting to hear that it was an empty threat from the good Catholics.

"Yesterday, they wrecked our secretary, Janet's, bookshop. She just sells general books, that's all. She's the nicest lady. But she is determined to come to this evening's soirée, and enjoy herself. Just to spite them. Elaine and I were at her shop early this morning, helping her clean up."

It shocked me to hear that a group of Catholics would do this. I wouldn't have believed that this type of thing would happen here.

"I am sorry to hear about your secretary's bookshop. But maybe, we should get back to the girls," I suggested, thinking that it might be better if Lettie and I kept away from their circle after today, which may be difficult, now that Lettie and Elaine already looked inseparable.

William grabbed me by the arm and then said genuinely, "Seb, let's have a good day."

There were only the conductor and a couple of passengers left on the tram, after we passed the huge Camberwell Junction, Lettie starting to tap her feet on the floor, giving away her nervousness.

When William and Elaine stood up, Lettie and I followed suit.

"Come on, Lettie. I'll show you how Aggy and I used to get the tram to stop at the closest street to our home. It's a bit scary. Do you want to have a go?"

Lettie nodded, without saying a word.

"You have to hold on tight to the pole and then step out onto the running board," Elaine insisted, with a cheeky grin on her face.

As the tram slowed, Elaine opened the sliding door, keeping an eye on the 'Connie' at the other end of the tram. Lettie and Elaine stepped onto opposite ends of the running board, holding on tight to the long metal poles. When they were settled, Elaine yelled out, "Make like a star".

Elaine stuck out her left arm and leg and then stretched out from the tram. Lettie did the same, following Elaine with a scream.

"STOP!"

The tram pulled up sharply, well before the tram stop I could see ahead, but exactly opposite Glyndon Road, where Elaine wanted to stop. The driver and conductor stuck their heads out from the front of the tram, asking what the bloody hell the girls thought they were doing.

The girls were still in fits of laughter when we turned right into Wattle Valley Road, a road which turned out to be something special in itself. I couldn't believe the large number of elegant houses lining either side of the street; all set on their own, surrounded by green manicured gardens, with what seemed like a new automobile in each driveway. It would take me thirty years, just to afford the car.

Elaine and Lettie went on ahead. Elaine eager to show Lettie her old room, before William and I got there.

"This is not who the Parmenters are, Seb. They'd be the same no matter where they lived," William explained, while looking at each house, somewhat in awe himself. "This street does have something about it, though."

This part of Camberwell was like a paradise compared to anywhere I'd lived or even seen before, it made sense for a family to want to raise their children here.

William turned right after a thick hedge, into a drive-way, I presumed Elaine's parents. I was immediately taken aback after clearing the hedge by just how big their property was, as big, if not bigger, than any of the proper-ties I'd seen so far in the street.

A large round lily pond was centred in the front yard, with a small fountain in the middle that poured water into a birdbath, the Parmenter's enormous pink stone house set perfectly behind it. A high, deep verandah supported by pillars designed in an upwardly swirling pattern, shaded the ground floor. The roof which rose to a point, well above the lower level, had at least four small framed windows jutting out on each side. This was the finest house I'd ever seen in my life.

From somewhere inside the house, I could hear the 'Charleston' being played only just louder than yelling and laughing. On the front verandah, William stood in front of a stained-glass double door adorned with native birds and animals, talking to a tall distinguished looking man who wore a bow-tie.

"Seb, come up and meet Mr Parmenter," William called out.

I suddenly felt weak. This man had done so much in his life, met so many interesting people. I was gripped by nerves, something so unusual for me. I had to steady myself to get up the steps and then over to Mr Parmenter.

"Mr Parmenter, this is my good friend, Seb. He's originally from the Wimmera, now Carlton."

"Pleased to meet you, Seb. I met your sister earlier. Our family spent a month camping near Avoca in the Pyrenees ten years ago. A wonderful part of the world. Does your family live nearby?" Mr Parmenter asked, putting out his hand to shake mine.

"Pleased to meet you, Mr Parmenter. We're on the other side of the hill, near Greens Creek. It is nice country ... the kangaroos and rabbits like it," I said, stupidly.

"I did notice that, Seb. Please call me, Blake. Mr Parmenter is such a mouthful."

He opened the right-hand side of the stained-glass door, urging us to go in.

"Let's see if we can't get that music turned down a little," Mr Parmenter shouted, forced to raise his voice, as the 'Charleston' made a repeat performance in the background.

The music and chatter grew considerably louder, when we turned into a large room, probably a dining room, a table and chairs pulled to one end. Three middle-aged women were lined up in the centre of the makeshift dance floor, doing their own version of the Charleston, their arms spread over the nearest shoulder, their legs struggling to keep up with the frantic tempo of the tune. William said that the tall lady in the centre was 'Gran' Sheriff, the most energetic woman in Melbourne, and a real force to be reckoned with. The skinny lady on her left was Janet Stomms, the lady who had her bookshop ransacked. She was small and I couldn't believe any God-fearing person could feel good about intimidating this thin, frail-looking lady.

William said the woman on Gran's right was Enid Parmenter, but I'd already cottoned on to that, Elaine was a spitting image of her, with one point of difference. Despite the dancing and laughing I could see a sadness in her mother's eyes.

The three women, who ended up overbalancing in their attempt to keep up with the Charleston, fell in a heap on the dining room floor, sitting up to hold each other, while they laughed their heads off. William said he would introduce me to Enid later, when she was more disposed.

"I promised you a beer, Seb, and that's what you'll get," William declared, heading deeper into the house.

William and I pushed on through a mass of guests mingling in a wide corridor, William talking to some, stopping to shake the hands of others. We left the interior of the house through another set of double glazed doors, onto the polished timber floor of the verandah, which seemed to surround the whole house.

On the left side of the verandah, a natural-timber laundry was discretely detached from the house, a concrete trough visible through an open door. Brown bottles sitting above the rim meant they must be on ice.

A small school of drinkers was already forming outside the laundry, when William flicked the top off a frost-covered bottle, pouring the golden amber into two glasses.

"Seb, try this and then tell me you've knocked down a better beer than Blake's home brew. I dare ya," William bragged, trying hard to make amends for his earlier behaviour.

Truly, a better beer I'd never tasted, and I didn't think

any beer would ever come close to the ones Lettie and I used to sneak from Dad. I'd have to get Lettie to try a glass later.

After we'd polished off the long necked bottle, William and I went for a wander amongst the guests, milling in groups around the oval-shaped backyard lawn, which was overhung with festive lamps tied between native trees and bushes, the sun starting to hide behind the rooftops to the west.

William eased his way into a group of five men, who he described beforehand as 'influential', leaving me to hang on the outside like a dag on a sheep. A large, gruff man, who looked like he'd had as many fights as feeds, held the floor.

"Those blood sucking real estate agents," the man said and then stopped to look around, "I hope there's none listenin' in, have finally got their comeuppance in Richmond. I thought those mugs would've given up on turfin' out families who're havin' a little trouble on the jobs front. But no, there's a new breed of mongrel that've moved in who've forgotten what happened in thirty-one. So, me and the boys from the Unemployed Workers thought we'd take 'em on a bit of a trip down memory lane, 'cept this time a couple of our watches were out of whack. By the time we'd unloaded a brick or two through some agents' windows, the coppers were right on our clacker. We only managed to lose 'em, when we split up and bolted like

Phar Lap down the pitch-black lanes of Struggletown," he said with his more than adequate belly heaving up and down as he laughed at his own story.

"The bloke next to him is the Federal Minister, Mick Whiteman. A very good man. His company has done more 'pro-bonos' than any other wigs in town," William whispered, while he had a sweeping look around the gathering, perhaps to look for Elaine.

William had lost me with his 'wigs' and 'pro-bonos', but I was beginning to understand why Aunty May called the Parmenters 'Prominent Australians' if they had friends like Mr Whiteman.

Just in the nick of time, Elaine and Lettie came to the rescue, saving us from the reminiscing of the 'influential' group. Elaine reached up and gave William a passionate kiss on the lips, holding him tightly around the waist, right in front of Lettie and me. Lettie looked away, as I did, confronted by the awkward reality that we didn't have anyone of our own. Lettie and I nodded to each other that it was time we went for a walk, to give these sweethearts a little space, and to see if there was anything to eat at this soirée.

As we passed a group of showy women who had commandeered the far end of the lawn, laughing louder than anyone else in the backyard, Lettie stopped, pulling me to one side.

"Grub," Lettie whispered, "I've seen that girl before — the one with the short black hair — just recent."

I looked over to see a sour-faced older woman with streaky blonde hair, plastered with tons of make-up, talking to three brightly dressed young women, two with short dark hair, one with long wavy red hair, all under tiny feathered hats, sipping on glasses of champagne.

"Which one. There's two of 'em?"

"The one next to the old biddy. Do ya see her?"

I took my time to look at this girl. I definitely had seen her somewhere before, as well as the other short-haired girl, but I couldn't quite put my finger on it.

"I know what ya mean, Lett. Don't know where I've seen her though."

The girl noticed me looking at her but didn't seem to take any offence.

"I know where, Grub. She's from the Children's Hospital. I talked to her yesterday; she's a volunteer. You should see how good they are with the children," Lettie said, really excited to see this girl. "Come on, we'll say hello."

Lettie was off, leaving me straggling behind, with the sole thought that maybe these girls were quite happy on their own. Lettie fronted up to the group, apologising and then asked the dark-haired girl in question, if she helped out at the Children's Hospital. The older lady immediately darted the filthiest look in Lettie's direction.

"Hi!" the dark-haired girl replied, in a high put-on voice. "Yes, of course I do. I could cuddle each and every one of those darlings to death, they are so beautiful. Did we introduce at the hospital, if not, I'm Clarisse, glad to meet you." The girl bowed, sticking out her white-gloved hand for Lettie to shake, which she did.

"I'm Lettie, remember. What a coincidence to run into you here," Lettie continued. "I have so much respect for the work you do with the children. I couldn't do it."

"I cried for the first week at the Children's, you know. Now, they give me so much strength. One day I hope to go to Spain to work with the poor and orphaned over there," Clarisse added, looking around at her friends. "All us girls do volunteer work for the Spanish Aid Committee, that's why we're here."

Then, after a second, "I'm also waiting on news for when I can start my nurse training. I want to go to Spain, so badly."

I wasn't sure whether Clarisse was innocently overdoing it or not, but anyone that gives up their time to care for children with polio has my respect.

The older lady pursed her lips, before saying, "Let's take the girls to get something to drink, Clarisse. More champagne, perhaps?"

I told Lettie after they'd left, that she had to come and try some of Mr Parmenter's home brew. But, before we could make it to the laundry, we were stopped in our tracks by the clinking of glasses and calls for silence.

Everyone looked over to see Mrs Parmenter standing in the middle of the lantern-lit verandah, waiting quietly for the murmur to die down. Enid turned towards her house, and then waved two people to come forward. A lady and then a man carrying a guitar, stepped onto the verandah, their heads held high with dignity. The woman dressed elegantly in a blue dress with a red and gold sash over her heart, the man in black trousers wearing a loose white frilly shirt, with a wide red sash tied tightly around his waist.

Lettie looked at me and said, "Wow!"

"Dear friends, I have two wonderful people that I would love you to meet this evening. They are on a goodwill visit to our fair shores, to show us the beauty of the Catalonian culture of Spain, something which Blake and I can personally testify to. Please make welcome, Señora Camila, and Señor Carlos Onetti."

Everyone clapped freely, as Carlos set himself on a chair, Camila stepping near the edge of the stairs that led down into the garden. Neither Lettie nor I expecting anything like this.

"Tonight, they will be playing and singing a traditional Catalan lullaby called, *El Noi de la Madre*, which if Camila and Carlos will permit me, translates as 'The Mother's Child'."

Only the rustling of leaves in the evening breeze could be heard as Carlos began slowly playing his guitar. When his wife started to sing, there was no need to understand the words, everyone knew this mournful song was about a mother's love for her child. During the song I caught a glimpse of Mrs Parmenter out of the corner of my eye, shaking uncontrollably as she was being held by her husband. I looked away, not wanting to imagine how much worse they would feel if they knew the secret that William and I were keeping.

Carlos and Camila received a huge round of applause at the end of their song, some guests cheering loudly, Long Live Spain ... *Viva España!*

Carlos stood up, bowing with Camila to the cheering crowd, as Enid came over to give Camila a kiss on the cheek, Blake shaking Carlos' hand.

"We feel so humbled by and appreciative of Carlos and Camila, that they have taken time out of their busy schedule, to play such a beautiful song at our soirée this evening. I know they must now head back into the city, but we hope they can take back with them to their homeland the love and support of the Australian people in their desperate hour of need. *No Pasarán!*" Blake yelled, raising his right fist in the air to the cheers of all the guests.

The party seemed to kick off after that, with everyone beginning to mix and let their hair down. Lettie and I finally managed to meet a much happier Mrs Parmenter, a lovely lady to talk to, so interested in Lettie and my life, even though her own worries mustn't have been far from her mind. Enid asked Lettie if she would like to help Elaine and her make teas and coffees for some of the guests, a fair excuse perhaps for Elaine and her Mum to get to know Lettie better, and to catch up on the latest gossip.

I gravitated towards the laundry, knowing that's where most of the blokes would be, close to the beer. William was there, talking to a tall, gawky looking fellow, who must have just arrived. The tall man, about the same age as William and I, was holding a beer bottle in one hand, a half-full glass in the other, and a rolly stuck out of the corner of his mouth. This was the type of bloke I was used to.

"Grab ya self a glass, young man, and we'll get ya lubricated," the tall bloke urged, as soon as I walked over to get in on their conversation.

I grabbed a cold glass and got back in a flash.

"Now, lean ya glass over, my friend. Ya don't want it spillin' all over the shop, do ya?"

"You're a lifesaver, mate," I said, before I took a long sip. "I'm Seb."

"I know, and I'm Charlie. Charles Hopes Esquire, that is. At your service," he announced, before bowing like a nobleman and then shaking my hand.

"Seb, this is the man the history professors go to, to get their articles edited. Can play a bit of cricket, too. Though, I suspect he uses it too often, as an excuse to avoid getting involved with the Aid committee. We love him anyway," William sprouted, his voice raised, perhaps enjoying Mr Parmenter's home brew too much.

"Bill, I think you've imbibed too much of Blake's beloved golden amber. I will be at the Bourke Street stand on Saturday, and, of course, I wouldn't miss out on the 'Spanish' debate, Monday week. So stick that in ya pipe, old fella," drawled Charlie, perhaps a little tanked himself.

"Which parties, unions or societies are you involved with, Seb?" Charlie asked. "If you're like Bill that would be about a dozen?"

"I'm not in any, can't afford it. Not allowed to anyway, my foreman would kill me," I replied, being a hundred percent honest.

"His foreman needs a visit from my twin brothers, hey Charlie," William chipped in. "They'd change his tune." He looked at me as if it would have only taken a nod to make it happen.

"I wonder if those twins are human sometimes, Bill, they're so big. They certainly would be handy around the campus at the moment, would scare the pants of those bloody Campeins. Pity they never sat the Merit Certificate!" Charlie added, knocking down his full glass of beer in one go.

"Let's go and see what's happenin' inside," William said, perhaps recognising he needed a breather from the homebrew.

Fortunately, someone had taken control of the gramophone, not allowing any more of the 'Charleston' to be played. One of my favourite big band tunes, Benny

Goodman's 'After a While' was playing at high volume as Charlie, William and I worked our way towards the centre of the house. I could even have a dance, if I found the right girl.

'Goody-Goody' had just been put on the gramophone, when we left the main corridor and headed into the former dining-room, where Mrs Parmenter and her friends had danced earlier in the evening. There were at least forty people on the packed dance floor trying to copy the latest swing moves, Elaine in the far corner of the room going through a pile of cylinders. I looked around for Lettie, but couldn't see her until the spin came around in the jive. Then, I saw her being twirled around by a man, an older man, on the far side of the room.

Of course, Lettie could dance with whoever she wanted, but I was just a little worried she mightn't know how to handle an older man, who is determined to get what he wants.

I stood watching Lettie, weighing up whether I should intervene or not, when Elaine grabbed me by the hand and led me onto the dance floor. I danced, or tried to dance, with Elaine until thankfully, William cut in, leaving me nothing else to do, but head outside to the laundry for a beer.

I thought it would be a wise move before I returned to the laundry and attempted to force more beer into myself, to make a small diversion to find a toilet. I wandered down an empty corridor on the left of the house, barely able to hear the commotion on the dance floor, until I reached two doors that stood side by side, usually a good sign that one was the 'toot'.

The door on the left opened outwards to reveal a large linen press. The door on the right opened into a small room that seemed to fit the bill, but due to the small amount of moonlight coming in through its lace-covered window, it was hard to tell. I felt around but couldn't find a cord to pull on or a switch to flick, to make me sure I was in the loo.

Outside the window, I could hear a muffled, but certainly unhappy voice. I peered through the lace curtain to see who was having a gripe. Under the verandah, leaning against one of the swirling pillars, was Clarisse with the sour-faced older lady, standing uncomfortably close to her.

"Clarisse, listen to me, please. Don't say a word," the older woman demanded and then placed a finger over Clarisse's lips.

"You are not going to Spain, or anywhere else. Do you understand? You are staying here and you are doing what I say. And if I hear any more talk about you becoming a nurse or leaving, your next job will be doing tricks for Spokes in his stinkin' hot tin shed in North Melbourne."

The older woman took her finger away from Clarisse's

lips, rubbing her shoulders gently, trying to appease her. Clarisse brushed her aside and moved to leave but was stopped abruptly by the older lady who raised her hand as if she was going to strike her.

Suddenly, the light came on in the bathroom. I wheeled around, surprised to see Charlie standing at the door staring suspiciously at me, his hand on a light switch high on the wall.

I wanted to tell Charlie what had just happened, but I remembered that my invitation to this soirée was built on the slimmest thread of coincidence, and any incident could reflect badly on Lettie. I didn't like the thought of her having to explain why her brother had been found loitering in a dark room.

I turned back quickly to look through the window, just as Clarisse looked up. I caught her gaze for long enough to see a deep embarrassment that I may have heard or seen what transpired.

"What are you up to, Seb?" Charlie inquired more than asked. "Doesn't matter, I don't wanna know. Mrs Parmenter is taking anyone that wants to go back into town, back into town. So, if ya wanna lift, ya'd better get on ya bike."

Charlie then stopped momentarily as he went to leave the bathroom, looking back at me as if he thought that I was perhaps a little peculiar.

Lettie was waiting for me, thankfully alone, on the

front verandah. I could tell she was having the best night of her life, so she didn't need to know what I saw through the bathroom window, no matter what I thought about it. It was just another secret I had to keep.

The guests were leaving en masse as Mrs Parmenter backed a huge Wolseley Straight Eight out of their garage. Lettie, then another girl, who I hadn't noticed during the evening, shuffled along the padded leather seat, followed by Charlie, then me, all comfortably fitting into the massive compartment that was the backseat of the car. The four of us said a big thank you through the rear window to Mr Parmenter, who was holding the fort until all the guests left. Elaine, then William, slid onto the front bench seat next to Mrs Parmenter.

As we backed out of the driveway, I could see Clarisse walking out through the stained-glass double front doors with the sour-faced woman holding her by the arm, all of their group speaking to Mr Parmenter.

Before we were halfway home, Lettie was fast asleep, her head leaning against the padding near the window. The other girl had fallen asleep as well, her head at an awkward angle against Lettie's shoulder. Charlie was wide awake, looking straight ahead, not interested in any more conversation. William and Mrs Parmenter chatted about the upcoming debate at the university.

"I'm worried about the Campeins stacking the audience in the lecture room, Mrs Parmenter, causing a huge imbalance in the fairness of the debate. And I know the Debating Society still haven't settled on a proposition for the debate, either. The last I heard they were planning to call it 'The Spanish Government is responsible for the current misery in Spain'," William informed Elaine's mum, respectfully waiting for a response.

"Provocative title, William, though I am glad to debate Spain on any terms, in any forum. If the Northern Lecture Room cannot provide a visible degree of fairness, we will ask that the debate be moved to a bigger venue," Mrs Parmenter replied calmly.

"Are Lettie and you, Sebastian, going to the debate? It should start about eight p.m. We may need the numbers," Mrs Parmenter joked, keeping her eyes fixed on the road.

"I don't know, Mrs Parmenter. We weren't sure if it was open to the public," I replied, thinking I could be too tired to listen to a heavy debate on a Monday night.

"The public are always welcome to the Debating Society nights. The usual attendance rarely warrants any more than a small lecture theatre, but not on this subject. I'm told there has been a huge amount of interest from outside of the university, as well as within. It would be lovely if Lettie and you could attend," Mrs Parmenter pressed, making it hard for me to refuse.

"I will ask Lettie tomorrow, but I'm sure we can make it, as long as Lettie doesn't have to work too late in the kitchen," I added, knowing we weren't going to get out of this.

It was probably well after ten, when Mrs Parmenter pulled the Wolseley up close to the gutter in Pelham Street, leaving Lettie and I only the shortest of hops to get across to Aunty May's. For the last part of our trip, the occupants of the huge cabin were happy to watch the buildings pass by in complete silence, tiredness having finally caught up with all except Mrs Parmenter, who seemed to have a boundless supply of energy.

I walked around the car and gently opened the door next to Lettie, who had begun to wake up. William hopped out of the car as well.

"Well, we got through it," William whispered to me, softly enough so no-one else could hear him, before helping me lift Lettie out of the car.

Lettie woke up enough to thank Mrs Parmenter and Elaine again for inviting us to their beautiful home and the wonderful soirée, I also thanked them and said we hoped to be able to do something for them in return one day. Mrs Parmenter responded that the only thing she wanted was for us to always be safe.

William helped Lettie jump across the gutter, saying that if we didn't have anything to do next Saturday, we should visit Elaine, Charlie and himself, and help out at the Aid stand, out the front of Myer in Bourke Street. If we had time, we could go for a coffee, afterwards.

"It's a date, then," Lettie called out, suddenly fully awake, as William hopped back into the car. Elaine waved to us through the rear window, before Mrs Parmenter gunned the motor of the Wolseley, which then sped off towards the university.

10

The Great Debate

On Wednesday evening, the flyscreen door of Aunty May's kitchen slowly creaked open, a hand holding a piece of paper slid past the frame and then began waving madly about in the air. Was this the good news we'd all been waiting for?

The next thing, Lettie jumped through the door, arms outstretched.

"I got it! I got it!" she yelled with a huge smile on her beaming face.

Aunty May sat still, unsure what this display from Lettie was all about, until suddenly realising that it was one of the biggest moments in Lettie's life, and everyone else's that cared for her. Lettie now had something concrete to build a new life on, a permanent job, something as rare as hen's teeth nowadays.

I ran over to Lettie, giving her a big hug and then Aunty May followed giving her a kiss on the cheek, saying she always had confidence that the job was hers.

I couldn't recall Aunty May ever saying that, but it didn't matter — Lettie had the job!

What a few weeks she'd had, we both had, but this was the icing on the cake, a real chance to get ahead down here. Everyone was looking for the same thing at the moment, to get some regular 'coin' coming in. It underlined everything.

Aunty May said she would cook up a huge leg of lamb for a special lunch for everyone on Sunday, and even buy a couple of bottles of beer for a real celebration of what she called 'Lettie's turn of luck'. She told Lettie and I that we could invite our new university friends over for the lunch, if we liked. But, Lettie said it was unlikely they would come, because Elaine and William were planning a big day on Sunday, in preparation for a university debate the next night, although she would make a point of asking them on Saturday afternoon, when we planned to meet at the Bourke Street Aid for Spain stand.

I was a little reluctant to tell Lettie, after her great news that I wouldn't be going with her into the city on Saturday. So I decided to leave it until Friday to let her know that I would be going with Lenny to a Carlton practice match on Saturday afternoon, straight after work. I didn't want to have to explain to her that I just wanted to get away from William, and the troubles surrounding him, for a while. I wanted to go somewhere where I didn't have to think.

After I told Lettie on Friday night, she just smiled, her head still in the clouds. "You can do whatever you want to, Grubby!"

Lettie did tell me later that night, she had planned to go clothes shopping on Saturday afternoon with Elaine anyway, but first had to sneak Elaine away from the Aid stand for long enough, to help her spend a fair whack of her first pay packet in Myer or Georges.

It was the right move, not to go into the city with Lettie on Saturday, not that I wouldn't have minded joining everyone for the coffee that William had promised, but I would only have ended up being bored to death, hanging around the Aid stand all afternoon, while William and Charlie went about parting shoppers from some of their 'hard-earned'.

Another reason I wanted to clear my head at the footy, was that I couldn't get out of my mind the image of that sour-faced woman, lifting her hand to Clarisse at the soirée last Sunday, and then to see the embarrassment on her face when she looked up at me.

I knew Clarisse was probably a working girl, and the older woman her 'Madam', but no-one deserves to be treated like a slave or threatened with violence. I wanted to help her, but where would I begin to start, and would she really want a young bloke, not long out of the bush, riding in like a white knight to rescue her. I doubt it.

In the end, Clarisse was the only one who could solve her problems.

*

On Saturday afternoon, it felt like we were already back in the middle of winter. I was shivering in a cold and lazy wind out the front of the Heatley stand at Princes Park with Lenny, eating a lukewarm meat pie with the tiniest dab of sauce on it, which I was lucky to get from the only concession stand open for the practice match.

The Bluebaggers were giving the hapless Royboys a fair touch-up, and it wasn't even half-time. But this was great, getting away from any dramas, if only for a short time. This afternoon wasn't going to get any more serious than wondering why the new coach, Rowe, hadn't taken Vallence off for a break and given some other poor bugger a chance to kick a bagful of goals at full forward. After all, 'Soapy' had already kicked eight.

I was told by Aunty May as soon as I moved permanently into her boarding house, that I had better barrack for Carlton from now on. "You want to fit in, don't you, Sebastian?"

The roomies were all big fans of the Navy-blue and would have, without doubt, given me no end of stick if I didn't join them. After the Blues had won the next six games in a row, I gave myself a pat on the back for the great choice I made. Unfortunately, I only got to one of the games.

Lenny was incredible with his statistics on the Carlton players, even the new ones. He knew their numbers, how many games they'd played, how many kicks they got each week. His speciality though, was goals, not only how many goals our players kicked, but against whom, and their career total. He also knew every other team's goal-kickers, as well. Lenny could rattle off figures for hours, if you let him.

My favourite player was full-back Jim Park, number twenty-six, who wasn't playing today, probably because he wouldn't have had anything to do. The only game I managed to see him play in was against a very determined Bulldogs outfit, in Round Sixteen the previous season. He kept Morrison down to two majors up until the end of the third quarter but Artie Olliver was playing a loose man in the forward line appearing to kick goals at will. Carlton were only two points in front with a couple of minutes to go, when the ball was kicked long into the Bulldogs' forward line. Park ran forward of Morrison and then backed back quickly into a flying pack. The umpire had no choice but to give him a free kick for a push in the back, or else the Blues fans would have rioted. He then took his time to kick long for 'Soapy' Vallence to goal just before the final bell.

I loved the way 'Gentleman Jim' outsmarted the opposition.

*

"Hang on, Lett, hold your horses," I yelled out as I saw her heading up the back stairs that led to my digs.

Lettie turned around halfway up the stairs and then pointed to a green velvet hat with matching feather, tilted at an angle on her head.

"Look at this, Grub," Lettie grinned, rocking her head to show it off. "Ya don't wanna know how much it cost. I got it at Georges."

"Lett, ya gotta keep a bit for 'ron, ya know. Aunty May's gonna want her board."

"Come on, Grub, you're allowed to splash out once in ya life. It was fun."

We headed up to the landing and then sat on the edge, with our feet stretched out over the steps, catching the last rays of the afternoon sun.

"How'd the footy go, Grub, Blues win?" Lettie asked, adjusting the angle of her hat again.

"Yeah, they killed 'em, an easy win. How'd the stand go today, make a bit a dosh?"

"Yeah, they had a good day. Clarisse and Charlie were helping William, so that made it easier for me to drag Elaine away to do some shopping."

"Clarisse was there?" I asked casually, trying not to act surprised.

"Yeah, didn't ya hear her say last Sunday, she helps out the Aid committee?" Lettie replied. "She hurt herself at the Children's earlier in the week though, tripped over something in the ward, but she's all right," said Lettie without concern.

"Did William end up takin' ya for the coffee he promised or was he just full of hot air?"

"I think you're a little jealous of William, Grub. He's always a gentleman around me."

Bloody hell, she doesn't know the half of him.

"After we helped pack up the stand, William took us all down through the Block Arcade to his favourite café, 'La Rubrique'. We squeezed into a tiny booth near the window like we were in Paris. I was very impressed when William and Charlie spoke French to the owner, ordering coffee and cakes for us. When the coffee arrived, it was in tiny cups with no milk and tasted horrible. I felt like asking for a cup of tea, but I didn't want to offend William."

William this, William that. Time to change the subject.

"So, how is Elaine going with her school studies?" I asked. "What's she studying, anyhow?"

"University, Grub, and she's doin' Modern History as her main subject. She says that Charlie has helped her out of trouble a dozen times in the past two years. He's a good bloke, Charlie. He asked how you're doin'. That's nice of him."

"Yeah, he's quite a character, isn't he, more like the blokes ya come across back home? Ya'd never guess he was a history genius."

"The only grumble for the day was Elaine saying that William was spending far too much time on Monday night's debate and not studying at all. She says he gets fixed on things and won't let up until he's the master of 'em."

I was just about to say to Lettie that it was time I got out of my work clobber before they walked to the copper on their own, when Aunty May poked her head out from around the corner of the house at the bottom of the stairs.

"Hello. Did you both have a nice day?" Aunty May asked, in a friendlier tone than usual.

"Yeah, I had a ..." before I could say 'good day', my foreman appeared at the bottom of the stairs as well.

What does that bastard want?

"Hi there. Did your Aunt tell you that we received a letter for you both — from your brother?" he stated as if he was the Post Master-bloody-General.

"Which one?" I snapped, thinking we didn't need the likes of him delivering our mail.

"Vern, it has on the back," Aunty May chipped in sheepishly. "It must be from Tiny."

"Tiny, he's never written a letter in his life. Not that I can remember," Lettie said, shrugging her shoulders and then heading down the stairs to take the letter from the foreman.

There was something funny about this — we needed to read the letter on our own.

"Bring it up here, Lett. We'll read it after tea."

I could see Lettie was reluctant to bring the letter up, looking disappointed that she couldn't open it straight away. But, she eventually conceded and came back up with the letter, handing it to me on the landing.

"Thanks for bringing us the letter. Special delivery," I said, smiling. "Well see ya downstairs for dinner, then."

I felt the flap of the letter; it was moist. Someone had steamed open the letter.

*

Dinner on Saturday night was a lot quieter than any dinner since Lettie had received the news about her job. Barry had thankfully gone out for the evening, leaving Aunty May, Lettie, a couple of roomies and me to sit in awkward silence during the meal. The only topic to talk about was the weird up and down weather Melbourne was having at the moment.

The highlight of the evening was when Lettie brought out a large bag of lollies she had bought from Myer for everyone to share at the boarding house. Aunty May doled out one lolly each, before pouring the rest into a bowl, putting a tea-towel over the top so they would stay fresh for after lunch tomorrow.

I teed up with Lettie to meet me in my room as soon as she could get away after dinner. Earlier, I had wanted to open the letter myself before I came down from my room, but it wouldn't have taken a genius to work out that there mightn't be much good news in it, so it was better that Lettie and I enjoyed a decent meal first.

*

"Come in" I yelled, as soon as I heard the knock on the screen door of my room.

Lettie came in quickly, firmly shutting the door behind her, before sitting down next to me on the bed, both of us leaning against the wall.

"Someone's opened the letter," I said bitterly, as soon as she had settled.

"Are ya sure? I know Aunty May's a sticky-beak, but ..."

"I'm positive, Lett. And, what the hell's that bloody Barry doing getting involved in our business? I hate that bastard!"

"That's not helping, Grub. Best to read the letter first — could be nothing."

The flap came open easily. The letter was written in pencil.

"Ya don't mind if I read it, do ya?"

Lettie nodded her approval, with a look that told me to get on with it.

The letter started off in the standard fashion, Tiny asked how everyone was, and how things were progressing on the jobs front. He wrote that Mum and Dad were in reasonable health, Dad's arm on the mend, and also that Dad had made a few quid by getting in with a bloke who needed somewhere to fatten up his poor-grade stock of sheep, which he had bought up north for a song. Then, he wrote that Robbie was in the asylum.

"What!' Lettie cried out, her hands coming up immediately to her face. "Robbie," she mumbled under her breath.

We sat in silence for nearly a minute before I continued reading, hoping there was something more in it to explain why this had happened.

Tiny wrote that Robbie had become increasingly aggressive with everyone, especially those who tried to take him away from his books, which were far too advanced for his school curriculum. He said everything came to a head, when a female lay-teacher tried to confiscate his favourite mathematics book during religious instruction, forcing him to read from the Bible. Tiny wrote that in the report they received from the principal he had his hand on the Bible as he blasphemed, before ripping out several pages and throwing the scrunched up paper at the shocked teacher.

When the teacher tried to stop him from ripping more pages, he slapped her on the face — hard.

Tiny thought the school board's decision to suspend Robbie was made hastily to appease a hysterical woman, who everyone in the area knew was fanatical about her preaching. When the woman made a complaint of assault to the police, they had nothing else to do but come out to the farm and ask Robbie some questions. The police were sympathetic at the start until Robbie started to scream at them, yelling that he wanted to go to his room to study. The police told the family they had only one choice to make, or he was going to be charged, so Mum and Dad voluntarily committed him. Tiny wrote that he told the folks he didn't agree with their decision, believing Robbie could be cared for better at home than in an asylum, where the screams of patients could be heard from outside the walls. He said it would probably mean a lot of work, but that's what families do.

Tiny requested, if at all possible, for Lettie and me to come home to try and convince Mum and Dad to fight for Robbie.

"Mum and Dad did the right thing," I blurted out.

"Shut up, Grub!" Lettie shouted back, before running out of my room and then down the stairs.

*

I woke up early in the morning unable to sleep. I had hurt Lettie, and I knew it. I just didn't think how badly the news about Robbie would affect her. This was a disaster for our family, an absolute bloody disaster!

I sat in the kitchen on my own with a cup of tea in front of me, the sun not even up. I read the letter over and over again, trying to figure out why I so readily agreed with Mum and Dad's decision, and not considered Tiny's point of view.

According to Lettie, the last time she was home, Mum and Dad were already struggling to cope with Robbie, and it would only get worse as they got older, especial-ly, if he needed extra care for the rest of his life. Tiny thought that if we all rallied around to help, Robbie's problems would disappear, but they wouldn't. At least one of us would end up resenting him. Lettie would never complain but it would be her that would be giving up the most, just as everything good was starting to happen for her.

In the back of my mind I knew there was something wrong with the way I was thinking. Then I suddenly realised I hadn't seriously thought about Robbie, for a very long time. Didn't I care about my brother, anymore?

"Mornin', Grub. You're up early," Lettie whispered, her eyes red and watery as she appeared out of the corridor that led to her room. "I couldn't sleep, either," before pull-ing up a chair next to mine. "Any tea left in the pot?"

I nodded, thinking that I couldn't treat my brother like he didn't have a chance at life, like the rest of us.

"I'm sorry, Lett. I was being selfish ... Sorry."

Lettie leant her head against my shoulder. "That's all right, Grub. We'll work it out."

"We'll find a way to look after Robbie," I assured her.

Lettie poured herself a cup of tea and then sat back quietly.

"We could both go back home at Easter, Lett. It doesn't give us much time, but we could do it," I said half-heartedly, knowing we only had five days.

"I need to go back to bed, Grub. I'll think about it. You can have my tea if ya want."

I sat in the kitchen drinking Lettie's tea, a million things running through my mind until the room got too bright and I couldn't stay up any longer.

*

I felt better about things when I woke up on Sunday morning for the second time. I lay in bed wondering why I thought five days wouldn't be long enough to organise two train tickets and pack a bag. We were actually lucky that Easter was just in front of us. It would give us four days off in a row that we wouldn't normally have and would find hard to get, even if I asked the foreman nicely.

Money was the problem. After board, Lettie wouldn't have much left of her first pay, after spending pretty well all of it on a green hat, and it would be very unlikely, if not impossible, to get any board money back from Aunty May especially after she had lashed out on lunch today.

I worked out with the bit of loose change I had in my bedside drawer and with our week's pay on Thursday thrown in, we probably had enough on our own to get home and then return to the city. Finding board for the week after had me worried.

I stretched out in bed, enjoying the rare opportunity for a lie-in, and concluded it must have been the foreman who had steamed open our letter; it had been written all over his face. I could imagine how Aunty May would have been on Saturday afternoon, all in a flap when the mail arrived and there being a letter from Tiny in the bundle. She would have been desperate to find out what was inside, seeing that he'd never written before, so something serious had to be up.

Barry would have acted like a hero, saying, "I'll get it open for you, May. They won't even know." Or was I thinking the worst of him?

*

Aunty May's special lunch turned out to be a lot of fun. All the roomies, including the foreman, banded together to wish Lettie the best of luck in her new position, singing 'For she's a jolly good fellow' and then giving her a toast. They were blissfully unaware that all the cheers might be in vain if events back home de-railed her 'turn of luck'.

Lettie was in a positive mood, like me, perhaps thinking that even though we were going home to make a difficult decision about Robbie, at least we were going home.

It had been nearly seven months since I'd seen the rest of my family. I felt the timing was right.

I worked out with Lettie that if I wrote a letter tonight, it should arrive home before Friday, letting the folks know that we'd be arriving at the Stawell Railway Station, sometime late Friday afternoon. There was even a little excitement creeping into the way we were planning this trip. I would go down to Spencer Street Station after work on Tuesday, buy two one-way tickets and then when we returned on Friday, purchase the return tickets. Not exactly a cinch, but it should work.

Later in the afternoon, we told Aunty May about the disturbing news in the letter. She seemed genuinely surprised and concerned about what had happened to Robbie, asking us to pass on her best wishes to the family and wishing she could come back with us, but that wouldn't be possible, she had far too much to do in the boarding house. We didn't bother asking if we could hold back our next week's board for a few days.

Aunty May reminded us that jobs like Lettie's didn't come along every day, and she should think very carefully about giving it up, on the off-chance that one day Robbie would be like we remembered him when he was young.

Lettie and I both agreed that we really could do without going to the university debate tomorrow night, as we both had plenty of sleep to catch up on. But, there was never really any doubt we wouldn't go, knowing how much effort Elaine and William had put into organising support for Mrs Parmenter's debating team. We couldn't disappoint them by not turning up.

*

Instead of meeting outside the King's College, Lettie and I planned to meet at a small lane just down from the main entrance at Tin Alley, which would take us into the centre of the Melbourne University campus.

It wasn't that deadly hot a day, but with the air almost wet with humidity, working in my stuffy factory turned out to be a real struggle. The little energy I had left was slowly draining away, as I walked at a snail's pace up Swanston Street, past the Women's Hospital, gradually closing in on our arranged meeting place in the distance.

I wasn't alone in my travels in the fading afternoon sun, a steady stream of men and women from all walks of life, many still in their work clothes, others dressed for an occasion, were heading in the same direction as me. Perhaps, some of these fine folk were attending tonight's Spanish debate.

A good distance ahead, a large group of students dressed in navy blue jackets with red insignia, turned as one into the campus at Tin Alley. I couldn't believe these poor buggers were being made to trudge around in heavy 'bags of fruit', on such a humid day. When the last of the group disappeared into the main entrance, I could see Lettie bringing up the rear, not in her work uniform, but in a light green summer dress.

"Hi, Lett. How'd ya go in the heat today?" I asked as we caught up, before moving off the footpath to let through the mass of people turning into the lane that led into the centre of the campus.

"It was shocking, Grub. Some of the girls were near exhaustion and would have had to go home if Madeline hadn't let them take lots of short breaks outside. She's not going tonight, but she let me freshen up at her house. I would feel terrible if I had to leave her, Grub," Lettie said quietly, looking washed out.

I allowed Lettie's comment to slip by, determined not to mention the difficult decision we had to go home and make at the end of the week. It would serve no purpose to go over and over the same arguments; there would be plenty of time for talk at Easter.

Lettie and I made our way towards the centre of the campus, surrounded by a growing throng of people who filed slowly past faculty buildings, now shaded by a mass of dark green foliage. The Debating Society may be getting a much better turnout tonight than they could have ever wished for.

A short distance ahead, the path split into two. Lettie told me to take the left and stay close to her, warning that the campus turned into somewhat of a maze through to the Northern Lecture Theatre.

The next second loud voices boomed out from behind.

"Make Way! Make Way! You hear me. *Make way!*"

Lettie and I tried to move off the path, but couldn't, the people in front of us had stopped too suddenly, turning to look in the direction of the sound. Leaving Lettie and I stuck, smack dab in the middle of the path.

Three policemen in white bobby hats, heavy black uniforms, their batons raised, ran past me on the left, three policemen shot past Lettie, on the right.

Lettie let out a startled, "Oh, God!" as they continued at the same steady pace between two buildings, before disappearing through an arched opening into a vaulted corridor at the near end of a large stone building.

"Do ya think there goin' to the debate?" Lettie asked, slightly shaken. "They couldn't be, could they?"

"Dunno, Lett, I wouldn't have thought so," I replied, uneasy at the sight of these policemen.

Lettie and I passed through the same arch the policemen had only minutes earlier, and then strolled along the vaulted corridor with the low sun flickering through pillars on our left, casting long shadows across the path ahead. Our eyes were drawn to an incredible red, ribbed ceiling above, momentarily making me think I could be in another place in time. Beyond the pillars was a quadrangle, which Lettie said was the same one that held the

'Peace' meeting, almost a fortnight ago. Several camellias across the courtyard were starting to bloom pink and white.

"That's where Margaret and Danielle were standing at the 'Peace Group' meeting, holding up the 'World Peace' banner," Lettie said, pointing to the open far end of the quadrangle.

A group was currently in that same spot, appearing from a distance, to consist of at least fifty young men and women praying in front of a man whose appearance was hidden under a white-hooded robe. The curved wooden staff he was holding gave him the allure of a minister or a priest, more-so as many of his followers were on their knees in prayer.

"How were the students during tea tonight, Lett?" I asked. "Did any of 'em have words?"

"No, they were all right, Grub. A little quieter than normal, if anything. Why d'ya ask?"

"Nothing, I just wondered," I replied, getting a tingle down my spine that told me something wasn't right here.

Directly in front of the arched exit from the Quadrangle Garden was a large rectangular door, recessed deeply into the intricate façade of another grey stone building. Lettie said this was the entrance Elaine told us to take if we wanted to avoid lining up for ages at the main entrance.

On the large rectangular door a hand-written notice

pinned into the wood stated that the Debating Society would like to apologise, but due to overwhelming public demand the first debate of the year had been moved to the Public Lecture Theatre. An arrow at the bottom of the page pointed left.

To our left a long queue of people waited quietly to enter the cover of an arch that jutted out from the same ornate building, a tall clock tower stood proudly behind.

The crowd outside was almost silent but from inside could be heard the dull roar of people yelling and stamping their feet, on occasion, the stomping appeared to be coming from above the building.

Lettie and I got pushed from behind several times, as we shuffled through a heavy wood and iron door, noticing a sign on the wall in brass lettering that read 'Arts Building'. Lettie looked up at me, I think for reassurance at the very second we were drawn into a crowd that moved and jostled us about like it had a will of its own, not letting us get anywhere near the door marked as the entrance to the Public Lecture Theatre. A deafening noise emanating from inside.

The crowd moved us on to another door, further inside the building, but another queue had formed at that entrance. I held Lettie by the arm, not wanting to lose her in the crush, leading her away from the pull of the crowd to a larger corridor off to our right, stairs leading to a higher level.

"If we can't find an entrance up there, we'll have to get out, Lett. It's chaos in here," I shouted as loud as I could, making sure Lettie heard me.

At the top of the stairs, to the right, was a small corridor leading to double wooden doors. The doors were open to give access to the rear of the theatre and less than twenty people lined up to get inside.

"In here, Lett," I yelled, sweat pouring off me, as we took our place in line. "Are you all right?" I was concerned the heat might be taking its toll.

"Yep," Lettie replied, with a look of determination on her face that said she wanted to see what was going on inside, just as much as me.

When we finally entered the theatre, the scene in front of us was truly unbelievable.

From the rear of the theatre, through to the bottom of the steep stairs, to the far left of the podium, all that could be seen was a moving mass of people, banners rising and falling, while flags of all colours were swirled in large circles by their chanting supporters below.

Blue flags with a white cross and white flags with red crosses that brought to mind the Crusaders of old, dominated the left of the chamber. Undoubtedly, the stronghold of the Catholic supporters, who according to small snippets gleaned from William, favoured the overthrow of the Spanish Republic.

Flags of all colours flew in the centre, a circle of green

and white, further to the right, likely to be those of the Peace Group. Margaret and Danielle sure to be somewhere in the mix.

Red flags, those of the Communist Party and Labor Club, of which William said he was a member, had formed into a tight, loud group on the far right, to support the Republican Government.

A large banner which read 'No Pasarán' stretched out in front of them, aimed conspicuously towards the opposite side of the auditorium.

People could be seen straining to see through the skylights and air vents on the roof of the theatre. The stamping of their feet creating a huge racket, dust and pieces of roof drifting down on the crowd below.

This was sheer madness!

"Grub, look. Is that Elaine down there waving up at us? It's hard to see anything in here," Lettie yelled, trying to point her out.

I panned across the lower section of the theatre, red flags blocking my view.

"Yeah, I see her, Lett. She's pointing downwards. I don't know why?"

Lettie had another look and then cried out, "She's saved us some seats, Grub, quick let's get down there."

We forced our way down towards Elaine through men and women, young and old, pressed against the wall, or blocking the steps. The crowd was becoming agitated as if waiting for the start of a football match, the only difference being that I had never seen a football crowd like this before.

"Let them through, please," Elaine yelled out several times to the large group of red flag-wavers, who were chanting, "No Pasarán! No Pasarán!" while blocking our way to get to the precious seats.

After a fair bit of pushing and pleading, we finally made it through to Elaine and then flopped down, exhausted in the two seats she had saved for us, Lettie sitting next to Elaine.

Elaine leant over to us, saying with a degree of excitement, "If you thought today was hot, tonight is going to be hotter."

Elaine told us William was in the staff room with the three speakers for the negative, the proposition for the night had been changed late by the Campiens to 'That the Spanish Government is the Downfall of Spain', and there was a rumour that the supporters for the affirmative had been let into the theatre early by someone in the Arts Faculty sympathetic to their cause, so they clearly outnumbered the supporters of the Republic.

"How's your mum, Elaine?" Lettie asked, looking a little concerned that the Catholics weren't going to turn the other cheek today, like they did at the Peace Group meeting.

"She's good, Lettie, she's seen worse than this in Spain,

although I've never seen anything like this on campus before. I don't know what people will think of us," Elaine said reflectively, obviously disturbed by the proceedings.

No sooner had Elaine finished speaking, than her mum made her way into the theatre through the bottom right-hand entrance, followed by two men dressed in white shirts and black ties. The supporters of the Republic cheered loudly and stood as one clenching their right hands into fists, chanting "No Pasarán!"

Supporters of the affirmative, in the majority on the roof, stamped their feet as hard as they could, trying to drown out the chanting.

"The bloke behind Mum is John Brasse. He was called in late to fill in for Bert Hubert, who became ill this morning. Brasse is from the Labor Club, he's a good debater, never gets rattled. The tall bloke at the back is Dr Dwyer, a fiery character, he's cut down many an opposition speaker," Elaine explained, describing them more like prize-fighters.

A roar went up in the theatre, followed by a large section of the crowd rising to their feet chanting "Long Live Christ the King!" as the white-robed man that was leading prayers in the Quadrangle Garden marched in, lifting high a banner that depicted a sheep carrying a white flag with a red cross on it.

The three men walking behind him received rapturous applause from the affirmative supporters as they entered the theatre.

"The first man. I can't be sure of," Elaine admitted "but I think he's their new orator, the young Campien, Richard Santorosso. I've heard he will end up being their flag-bearer in the future. The next two blokes I know too well, both fascists: Neale and Jorgensen. Neale was asked to leave a meeting held by Margaret and Danielle two weeks ago."

"Yeah, I was at that meeting, Elaine. He seems like a strange bloke to me," Lettie broke in, showing more interest in the debate than I thought she would.

"They call him 'Toro the Bull' on campus because he tries to bully his opponents," Elaine joked, with a wry smile on her face.

An obviously uncomfortable young man in a blue gown stepped onto the small podium and then over to the lectern that had a microphone set to the side of it. Barely audible, he welcomed all on behalf of the University Debating Society, to the first debate of the year, through the cheers and boos of the audience. He read out the proposition and introduced the first speaker for the evening, Mrs Parmenter for the negative, and then left the podium.

Elaine's mum walked confidently up to the lectern, the crowd showing a degree of respect for her by quietening their brouhaha.

Mrs Parmenter started off pleading with the audience to understand that a newly elected government deserved the right to fulfil its agenda, without interference from a disgruntled aristocratic class and their military henchmen who had lost their privileges due to the election of a democratic government. She received an ovation from the Republican supporters around us, who loudly cheered and chanted while the affirmative supporters remained surprisingly quiet.

When Mrs Parmenter said it would take a long time for Spain to overcome the burden of hundreds of years of repression, the Catholic supporters for the affirmative seemed to take this as a personal insult. The speaker Jorgensen immediately jumped onto the podium, accusing Elaine's mum of hypocrisy, saying that Franco was fighting for democracy for all, not for anti-Christians and anti-Libertarians.

His supporters erupted into a cry of "Long Live Christ the King!" that drowned out Mrs Parmenter's response.

I looked around amongst the supporters loyal to the Republican side, wondering why William wasn't close by the negative speakers. I eventually saw him near the exit door, standing on the right next to a rough looking bloke.

"Who's that bloke with William?" I asked Elaine.

Elaine had to look around a few times herself before she could see them both.

"That's Madeline's husband, the cane cutter. He only arrived back in town a couple of days ago, looks shifty to me. I'd be wary of him, Seb," Elaine said with surprising certainty.

I would have bet all I had that a bludger like him wouldn't show his face again.

Jorgensen finished his tirade by saying that the Spanish Civil War was a fight to the death between two completely opposite philosophies: one totally reprehensible, the other the most inspirational institution in the world, the Catholic Church.

A middle-aged woman sitting in the centre of the theatre became so incensed by these comments, that she took it on herself to direct insult after insult at Jorgensen, at the same time as I caught a glimpse of Charlie sitting amongst the green and white flags of the Peace Group, writing something down.

When a group of young women started to shout down the outraged middle-aged woman from the affirmative side, she moved across to them, grabbing the handbag of one of the opposition's women and emptying its contents in a spray over the Catholic supporters behind her. She went again and again for other handbags, forcing two of the constabulary to move along the row, and then drag her bodily from the theatre.

Dr Dwyer leapt to the podium, out of turn in an attempt to recover the momentum that seemed to be slipping towards the affirmative. He pointed directly at the Campien, Santorosso, seated behind him.

"The Church has supported the habitual persecution of the poorest people in Spain. I say, don't deny these people their freedom." His voice lowered to a plea, "Let them be free. Let them be free." Then suddenly louder he demanded, "No country has ever been hurt by refusing the Catholic Church."

Fighting broke out in the middle of the theatre, near the Peace Group, as the new zealot Santorosso approached the lectern. He raised his arms, calling for all supporters of Jesus the King to heed his call.

"It is no longer necessary to render to Caesar the things that are reserved for kings and leave God the spoils of lesser deities. Our God is the king of all. *Viva Cristo Rey! Viva Cristo Rey!*" The Catholic supporters in the crowd rose as one to join him in a chant that drowned out all others in the auditorium.

What is he trying to say? Does he really want the Catholic Church to run the world? It just doesn't make sense.

I wasn't sure if I was dreaming when I felt cold spots of water on my arms, and then my face. I looked to my right, to see what looked like a misty rain falling gently over Lettie and Elaine. Near the bottom right entrance of the theatre, a group of five young men were directing a full flow of water from a fire hose towards the centre of the red-flag waving supporters of the Republic.

I saw William move quickly to grab and then wrestle one young man away from the back of the hose, throwing him to one side, before going back to try another. Elaine saw him and screamed out, "William don't, don't start a fight. Don't!"

I tried to push past a tangle of people on Elaine's right, and work my way down towards William, to try to pull him away from the scuffle but I was blocked by a wall of red-flag wavers surging down onto the group still managing to direct a snaking spray of water at their opposition.

Madeline's husband pulled the nozzle away from the young man at the front of the hose and then threw him heavily into the aisle, beating him several times to the face as he lay on the steps. A large red-faced policeman grabbed Madeline's husband in a headlock from behind, pulling him away from the young man still prostrate on the stairs; a second, and then a third policeman required to drag his thrashing body out of the theatre.

Someone had thankfully managed to turn the water off, but scuffles continued outside the auditorium. I found William making fresh air swings at a large bald-headed man with a wooden cross hanging in front of his chest. The superior reach of the big man's left arm was holding William at bay long enough until he could get a tight grip on the senior's ripped white shirt, before pulling him steadily into range and landing a good right to the left side of William's face.

From where Lettie and I had entered the Arts Building,

three policemen were wading into the crowd, heading steadily in our direction, aggressively throwing anyone that showed resistance behind them into the arms of other coppers, who then manhandled them outside.

I whacked down hard on the left arm of the bald-headed man still holding William's bloodied collar, allowing William to break free of his grasp to have another fresh air swing at him. The good Christian used some pretty decent swear words to describe us.

William and I made our way back inside the theatre to make sure Lettie, Elaine, and her mum hadn't become involved in a fracas, the cries of 'Viva Cristo Rey!' still echoing strongly throughout the theatre. My greatest worry at the moment was that the roof appeared to be flexing under the weight and pounding of the mass of Catholic supporters in the level above. I had to get Lettie out of here.

On the opposite side of the room, William and I could see Lettie, Elaine and Mrs Parmenter being led up to the back of the theatre by a man who looked a lot like Neale, the speaker for the affirmative. William and I forced our way up the stairs on our side of the theatre and then moved across the top row of seats, from where we could see the pandemonium unfolding below.

Charlie's height gave him away, as he held open the bottom left-hand exit door to let Margaret and Danielle pass through, their heads bowed. The modern day

Crusaders for the affirmative looked like they'd over-whelmed the infidels.

We caught up with Lettie, Elaine and Mrs Parmenter shortly after they exited through two wooden doors into the relative quiet of a hallway, on the opposite side of the theatre to where Lettie and I had entered earlier.

"Is everyone all right?" I cried out as I went straight over to Lettie, who nodded that she was fine. William, who was following close behind, ran up to a visibly upset Elaine, and her mother. Neither spoke as Elaine reached for a handkerchief in her handbag, and started to wipe the blood off William's face and neck.

"We're all right, Sebastian," Mrs Parmenter replied. "We thought in this instance, discretion would be the better part of valour and we should leave. I'm so grateful to Mr Neale for leading us through troubled waters." Mrs Parmenter nodded appreciatively to the opposition speaker. It only occurred to me now that Mr Parmenter wasn't with his wife tonight.

"Nothing that any good Catholic wouldn't do in the same situation, Enid," Mr Neale replied, bowing his head, before opening the two wooden doors to let out the victo-rious chants from within, and then closing it again, as he went back into the theatre.

We followed Mrs Parmenter, who said she knew how to reach the quadrangle entrance that Lettie and I had tried to enter earlier in the evening.

On leaving the Arts Building as a group, relieved to be away from the upheaval and able to breathe in the cool night air, we could still see a lot of activity around the arch-covered entrance to the Public Lecture Theatre, another poor unfortunate being dragged away by the police as we watched.

"I think Madeline's husband, Leo, was arrested. I saw him being dragged out of the building by three big coppers, after he sorted out the bloke directing the fire hose," William declared, surprisingly concerned for a man he must have only met in the last couple of days.

There was no response, which showed the lack of regard for Madeline's husband.

"We'd better tell, Madeline," I said eventually. Lettie and Elaine nodded in agreement.

Mrs Parmenter said she wanted to go back inside to find out how her fellow speakers, Brasse and Dr Dwyer, were faring; she was worried they might have become involved in a fight. William told her that she needn't worry, he had seen them in much worse situations than this on the docks, but he would go back inside to check, if that eased her mind. I'm sure he anticipated the affirmative supporters' euphoria would soon wane.

William suggested to Elaine and her mum that if they went to tell Madeline about her husband's possible arrest, he would join them shortly back in the Junior Common Room. Elaine's mum reluctantly agreed that

William was right but urged him to avoid confrontation, at all cost.

Lettie and I understood that we couldn't do any more now, except get in the way, and probably should be getting back home anyway, as the clock on the tower was showing well past eleven o'clock and we were almost a spent force. Mrs Parmenter told us that if we wanted to wait until William came back, she would be happy to drive us back to our aunt's. We thanked her, but told her we would enjoy a walk home in the fresh air.

Mrs Parmenter apologised to us for how violent the night had become and said she regretted putting Lettie and me in the way of danger. I was about to say in no way was it her fault, when Lettie jumped in looking quite emotional, saying although she was a little scared, the greatest shame of the evening for her, was that there was no debate.

Lettie said she would have loved to hear both sides of the argument debated openly, even ask questions of the speakers, and that the University may have lost a great opportunity to bring all the groups together to release some of the tension she has felt around the campus, from the day she walked in to see the 'Peace Group' meeting.

Everyone agreed wholeheartedly with Lettie's sentiments, but William added that unless the situation in Spain changed overnight, it would be a very long time before these rival camps embraced each other.

Lettie and I waved to our new friends while saying goodnight, before walking back through the arched entrance to the Quadrangle Garden, the cries of '*Viva Cristo Rey*' disappearing completely not far along the vaulted corridor.

11

Taking Stock

"The Vice-Chancellor is in big trouble at the Uni, Grub," Lettie came out with all of a sudden, before sitting down next to me at Aunty May's small kitchen table.

She said Madeline had told her the Vice-Chancellor had been summoned to face the Chancellor and the Board of Management to explain how he could have allowed the Spanish debate to proceed, when every indicator pointed to a complete debacle.

"Madeline reckons they will keep at him until he resigns," Lettie added nonchalantly.

My mind had only begun to clear three days after the event, allowing me to make some sense out of what had happened on Monday night. I couldn't believe the contempt the opposing groups held for each other when, in the end, they were only expressing ideas. It was a real eye opener to see how easily people can be drawn into taking sides, and then turn on anyone who doesn't agree.

"The College grounds and the Uni campus were like ghost towns during the week, Grub," Lettie added with a smile. "I don't think anyone's willing to show their face, in case they get recognised by someone who saw their bad behaviour at the lecture theatre. Everyone in the kitchen reckons that the five blokes who turned on the firehose will get suspended. If they can find 'em!"

"I'm sure everyone in the Uni knows who they are, Lett, except the big wigs. No-one will dob them in."

Lettie said Madeline had troubles of her own on Tuesday morning, angry that she had to leave the college kitchen for several hours in order to post her husband's bail at the Russell Street Police station.

"She called him every name under the sun, not all under her breath before she left. She says he's gone from being an ordinary bastard, to a real bad bastard," Lettie giggled.

"Leticia, what are they teaching you in that kitchen?" Aunty May huffed, shaking her head. "Can you come and get the kettle please, if it's not an inconvenience."

"Heads will roll for sure, Grub. Dunno how many though," Lettie declared, before getting up.

I didn't think Easter could come quick enough for the University of Melbourne.

*

Later that night, Lettie and I were enjoying the best cup of tea from Aunty May's silver teapot while she busied herself damping down the Aga for the night. The reality of our trip home tomorrow was beginning to sink in, when a face appeared in the darkened frame of the screen door, and softly called, "Hello?"

It was William's voice.

"William, is that you? Don't be like a stranger, hangin' out there. Come in," Lettie insisted jumping up to get the door. "What brings ya 'round these parts?"

"Just popping in for a quick visit, Lettie. How is everyone?" William asked jovially, conspicuously holding a book in his left hand.

It occurred to me that neither William, nor Elaine for that matter, had ever been into Aunty May's and our home, or had met Aunty May before. This could be interesting.

Aunty May threw off her apron and patted down her hair and dress before William had a chance to look over and notice her.

"Hello, you would be Lettie and Seb's aunt, if I may be so forward. They have spoken of you often, in glowing terms. Glad to finally meet you," William said charmingly, laying it on thicker than necessary, but exactly how Aunty May would have liked it.

"I doubt that my young charges would have said that, William. Please call me May. I am so glad that Sebastian and Leticia have been able to make friends with such generous and substantial young people as Elaine and yourself. Much has been recounted about the wonderful evening they spent at Elaine's parents' house in

Camberwell. I felt a little jealous, not attending myself," Aunty May gushed, turning a little red in the face.

"The next soirée the Parmenters have, I will personally make sure Elaine places you on top of the list, May. But, I do have a mission this evening. I found a book, as I was shuffling through my wardrobe this afternoon that I thought Lettie may like to read on the train or at Easter. It's my favourite of Blake Parmenter's books *Men Are Human, Too!*"

Aunty May interjected, "I've read that book, William. In fact, I have a copy somewhere in my room, such a witty book. He must be a clever man. Would I be correct, William?"

"He's a very down to earth man, May, great to talk to. Can't say anything bad about him, of course."

"Of course you can't!" laughed Aunty May as if she was Madam Pompadour.

After flattering Aunty May, William turned to me and asked if he could have a word with me outside, before going back to the college.

"Lovely to have met you, May, and I hope you enjoy the book, Lettie, but I must have a word with Seb," William apologised, holding the fly-screen door open for me.

"Sure will, see ya soon, William," Lettie smiled and then as she waved. "Please take care."

William returned a tiny smile back to her.

"Pleasure to meet you, William. I hope you can bring

Elaine around one day. I would love to meet her as well," Aunty May requested, her voice rising as William headed backwards out the door.

"I will make sure of it ..." William called back, closing the screen door while I tentatively followed him out to the back of the boarding house.

"Let's go down the lane a little, Seb," William said without emotion.

"Sure," I replied. We moved out of the glare of the only street light in the vicinity, to the shadows under a peppercorn tree, in the laneway at the rear of Aunty May's.

"I'm going, Seb, I'm going to Spain," William said, becoming quite jittery. "I have to, but I'm not going to fight. I'm going for another reason. I told you already about the rumours coming out of Spain."

I hoped for Elaine's sake that I was never going to hear those words, but in the back of my mind I also knew that it was only a matter of time.

"William, no, ya talkin' rot. Don't do it to Elaine," I pleaded. "With what's happening with her sister, she will be devastated. Don't be a bloody fool," I said, trying my hardest to convince him it was a terrible mistake, but not having any effect on his demeanour.

"Don't disrespect me by saying that, Seb. I'm trying to save Aggy's life. When I told you Agatha was amongst four women under suspicion for being a spy, I didn't tell you the whole truth ... She's the only woman under suspicion. The

Provisional Government only gives suspected spies so much time to prove their innocence. Then, they lose patience."

Why didn't Agatha just leave with her family?

"Listen, William, think about Elaine, how would she be if you were captured or killed?" I argued, walking back into the streetlight.

"I have no intention of being captured or killed, Sebastian. I'll be travelling with a high-ranking figure in the Seamen's Union, a Kiwi called Kernot who worked out of Barcelona for several years in the merchant navy. He has many contacts with local Government officials, and we have documents and letters to clear this up. I am not going into this blindly. To do nothing in this matter would be negligent and make a coward out of me," William said firmly, as he joined me under the streetlight.

"The suspicion came about when the Provisional Government was informed that the family Agatha was billeted with in Rome during her Red Cross training, had a son in the O.V.R.A, the Italian Secret Police. In all her letters from Rome, Agatha only mentions two daughters, and they and their parents were vehemently opposed to the fascist government, so it cannot be the same family. It's a horrendous error, Seb. I have to correct it," William explained, looking exasperated, feigning a kick at the wooden paling fence.

"When are you leaving, William?" I asked, resigned to the fact that nothing was going to change his mind.

"I don't want to tell you when, or how Seb, because I want you to leave with me," William declared, standing squarely in front of me. "I need you with me. You're the only person I can trust to have my back, all the time. You can tell me who to watch out for over there."

William looked at me with an expectation that I would jump at it.

"No, William, I can't. I want to help Elaine's sister, but I can't. I have to go back home tomorrow to decide what to do about my brother, Robbie. I have to give him priority at the moment. He is stuck in an asylum that only horror stories come out of. Lettie and I have to look after him," I tried to explain, becoming frustrated that I had been asked to choose between my family and someone else's.

"You're not his father, Sebastian ..."

"I know, but I am his brother," I said simply back.

William started to walk off and then turned around.

"You're a great bloke, Seb. But you will never grow up staying here. You will always do right by others, but not yourself. You can stay and work at Cooks for the rest of your life. Who cares? No-one will ever say that's when Sebastian made his mark. That was his day. All people will say is, how could he have put up with that stinking place for so long? He was better than that. They won't praise you for being strong, they will laugh at you for being weak."

William walked deep into the lane, returning soon after with a large canvas bag.

"People only judge you on what you do when it matters. I know you love Lettie and your family, but they're not you. Don't look back twenty or thirty years down the track and then realise that this was your chance, maybe your only chance, to decide where your life takes you. Help me bring Agatha back home to her family. Don't throw this moment away, Seb."

William continued to look at me for some time, and then walked to the end of the lane, not turning around as he disappeared out of the streetlight into the night.

I moved into the shadow of the peppercorn tree and leant my head against the wooden paling fence, knowing I would never see William again.

*

"Grub, are you there?" Lettie called out from the back steps of Aunty May's.

How could I hide the disappointment I was feeling? I had let down a friend who asked me to help save someone's life. I wanted to tell Lettie what had just happened, but that would only put her in the same dilemma as me; wanting to support friends that had already set themselves on a path, well before Lettie or I arrived on the scene.

"Out here, Lett. Just enjoying the fresh air," I called back from under the peppercorn.

"You're a strange one sometimes, Grub, it's freezing

out here. Is William still around?" Lettie asked, as she stepped out into the streetlight with a cardigan over her shoulders, probably wondering why I was still hanging around in the laneway with a cold wind starting to bite.

"He's gone, Lett," I replied, fighting a waver in my voice. "Back to the college, I suppose."

"Inside the book were two notes. One's nice, the other ... I dunno. William left a note saying how much he cherished our friendship, and how he loved to watch Elaine and I get on so well. He is a nice guy, ya know."

"I do know that, Lett. Who's the other note from?" I asked. "Ya don't have to tell me if ya don't want to."

"Now, Grub, don't get angry, but it's from the man I was dancing with towards the end of the night at the Parmenters. He wants to take me out to a dance, or elsewhere at a time of my choosing. I thought I'd let you know that I might take him up on it, if I get back," Lettie explained, giving me her best girly look, with her head leant to the side.

"The old bloke, Lett, he could be our dad. You don't know anything about him."

"I know he's just turned thirty, never been married before and he seems really nice. I like him, Grub."

"That's up to you, Lett, but I'll be watching him like a hawk. Ya know that?" I replied, not angry, just glad to have Lettie to talk to at the moment. "Let's go inside, it's gettin' too cold out here."

I moved out of the shadow of the peppercorn with my head bowed, trying not to show my face. Lettie stayed her ground.

"When's he leavin', Grub?"

"Who, Lett?"

"William. Sometimes ya don't give me much credit. I see more than ya think I do. It's what his life revolves around. He didn't come over to give me a book with a couple of notes in it. He came to ask you to go with him, didn't he?" Then Lettie looked at me closely.

"Are ya goin'? I won't blame you if ya do."

I looked at Lettie knowing that I had been treating her like a kid ever since she arrived in the city. I kept forgetting she was eighteen; already a young woman.

"No, Lett, it's something William has to do. Elaine's sister is in trouble, perhaps more trouble than any of us know. Lett, please don't go and tell Elaine that he's going to leave, it won't make a stitch of difference to what's gonna happen."

Then, I tried to explain to Lettie, the best way I could, that getting Robbie out of that asylum is all we should be concentrating on at the moment.

"Grub, Elaine's no fool. She knows one day William won't be in the dining room for breakfast. She told me that when we were on the tram to Camberwell. She'll be a mess for a time but she is surrounded by people who follow their convictions. I wish William had never come around here. I wish he had just gone…" Lettie said starting to cry.

I took a step towards her, but she walked away from me and then out of the lane. I followed Lettie to make sure she was all right, keeping my distance, not realising how much she cared about William. She stopped after a while, telling me to take it slow on the way back home, neither of us wanting to show Aunty May how upset we were.

*

Reading Mr Parmenter's book *Men Are Human, Too!* turned out to be the best medicine Lettie could have taken, as we whiled away the long hours on Good Friday, in our more-than-comfortable carriage on the giant 'Spirit of Progress' locomotive. Lettie said the insights shared by Blake Parmenter into the funny way people behave with each other were so revealing and hilarious at the same time.

Our soft seats and the motion of the train, allowed us to drift off into the deep sleep that neither Lettie nor I, had been able to find the previous night, or for many nights before that. After we woke, all we could think about was the drama that would be playing out in the student dormitories of the King's College at the same moment. The reality would have dawned upon Elaine in the morning that William had gone. He would have left a letter, one that I hoped went some of the way in explaining why he was hurting her so much.

Lettie and I hated the fact that we were even put into this situation, knowing that whatever we did it was never going to be right. In the end, we made the right decision to let Elaine and their friends sort it out on their own. William was set on a course now that would be difficult to change anyway. Most likely, sitting in the damp hold of a steamship heading out to sea, surrounded by like-minded souls; all looking toward an uncertain future.

At least all the thinking about William and Elaine had given us a reprieve from what we might be facing back home. I had to tell myself time and time again not to open up my big mouth and give an opinion unless it was really necessary, when the family gathered to talk about Robbie. I had stuck my foot in it with Lettie last Saturday, only barely managing to make things right, so I really didn't want to do it again back home.

For some reason, William's comment about me not being Robbie's father kept repeating in my mind. He really was a piece of work. It was good enough for him to trek to the other side of the world for his girl's sister, so why should he make me feel guilty about coming home to look after my brother.

Lettie and my concerns about home were instantly swept away when the 'Spirit' slowed in its approach to the Stawell Railway Station. We stepped out onto the smaller-than-I-remembered platform to see Tiny, Mum, Dad and Robbie waving madly at us from under the canopy of the old colonial-style station building.

"Robbie!" Lettie yelled out dropping her full canvas bag on the spot and running flat out towards him. She almost knocked Robbie over as she picked him up in one motion and spun him around and around, oblivious to everyone else.

"How ya doin', Grubby?" Tiny asked in his remarkable and familiar deep voice as I approached. "We got a bit o' good news for you and Lett." He grinned as he nearly crushed my hand in his massive paw.

"I can see that, Tiny. We didn't know what to expect after your letter," I replied, relieved to see Robbie surrounded by family.

Tiny picked up Lettie's canvas bag as if it was a feather and then we headed over to Mum and Dad, who were also being squeezed to death by Lettie. She was letting out every ounce of emotion that had built up inside her since she arrived in the city nearly four weeks ago.

I grabbed Robbie myself and gave him a big hug and roughed up his hair, before asking if he had been looked after in the asylum. He said he was happy in there, because he could study all day, but now, all he wanted to do was go home to study, which I said sounded like a damn good idea to me.

I gave Mum a hug and then shook Dad's hand. They

said they were doing well, and had news for Lettie and me, but didn't describe it like Tiny did, more like they were holding something back in reserve.

We all piled into Tiny's old Chevrolet Superior that had been converted into something resembling a rough take on a farm carry-all. The makeshift seats were hard on the bum and a terrible smell was seeping out of the boot, but there was nothing better than seeing Lettie with her arms around Robbie, who had started to sing an old sea shanty, which he must have picked up in the asylum; so grateful things were different to what I had expected.

*

It was late when we arrived back home at the farm, Robbie heading immediately into his room, which left the rest of us the opportunity to talk about his ordeal. Dad did the perfect thing and brought out a cold bottle of his favourite Abbots Lager. We each found our place around the lace covered dining room table, Dad pouring a glass of beer for all except Mum, who said she would make herself a pot of tea in the kitchen.

"I can't tell ya how good it is to be home," I said leaning back in my chair, finally able to relax. "Things have been like a roller-coaster in Melbourne lately, not all of it has been bad, though. What do you reckon about it, Lett?"

"I don't know how much Aunty May has told you," Lettie said to Dad. "But, Seb helped me get a job at Melbourne Uni, in the kitchen of the King's College with a lovely lady called Madeline. She's helped me settle in along with some other college students, Seb and I have met. My first pay packet helped too."

Lettie had a sip of her beer and then hopped up to see if Mum wanted help in the kitchen.

"May writes quite often, Seb and tells us things. Most of which, we don't want to know," Dad murmured, making me wonder exactly what Aunty May had put in these letters. "She reckons that you and Lettie are moving in different circles down there. I just hope you know what you're doin'. It can be a trap for the unwary."

"Dad, there's no way we could forget who we are," I replied, slightly annoyed. "Aunty May would make sure of that, she'd soon tell us if our heads got too big ... and you told me, never owe people money."

"I don't like to say too much in front of your mum," Dad whispered. "But, Vern and I have had to call in every favour we were ever owed to get us through the last few months, including to ask John Minacke, our local insurance assessor, who thankfully I used to play footy with, to give us something for the truck. He stuck his neck out a long, long way to get us enough folding stuff to put us near the black."

It appeared that things had turned around enough for

Lettie and me to be able to return to the city on Monday, without having to worry about the folks for one, but I'd been around for long enough to know that things were never that simple.

"What's the good news, Tiny?" I asked. "I'm in suspenders."

Lettie and Mum returned to the dining room as Dad began to explain the complex turn of events.

"After we were forced to place Robbie in the asylum, we didn't know what to do. All we could do was hope that vindictive bloody preacher woman dropped her complaint to the police, but there was little chance of that. Fortunately, Robbie was settled into a dormitory with boys his own age at Annadale, and he says he was quite happy in there, completely unaffected by the screaming and yelling of patients from buildings nearby.

"When we visited Robbie last Sunday, there was a group of doctors or the like, being shown around Robbie's ward, talking to most of the boys, appearing likely they were being organised for something. Vern got a bit annoyed that they were ignoring Robbie, so he went up to the doctor who seemed to be in charge, asking him why he didn't involve Robbie in all the fuss."

Then, Tiny jumped in, talking loudly over Dad.

"I fronted him about Robbie, but this bloke wouldn't take a backward step. He said he had to get a new special school up and running at Peaceful Creek within a week, and wouldn't be put off by anyone or anything. He introduced himself as Dr Lesser, a child psychiatrist, and went about explaining the school's aims and how he and a small group of colleagues had developed a new strategy for getting the best out of students with difficulties. He won me over completely when he said he would be living in a dormitory next to the new children's ward at the hospital, and wouldn't leave the kids unless he absolutely had to."

"He does seem like a solid man, Vern," Dad said, taking charge of his story again.

"The psychiatrist told Vern there were several reasons why he wasn't taking Robbie with him, not the least being that the police didn't want him to leave, but the main reason was that he wanted time to assess Robbie's condition at length, saying he wasn't sure if the asylum should have accepted him at all."

Dad took a solid swig of his Abbots before continuing.

"The doctor said he had attended a seminar in Germany early last year, where there was an overall fear of being able to speak freely about psychiatric patients, which the ruling Nationalist-Socialists considered sub-human, but he said a young Austrian psychiatrist wasn't afraid to speak to anyone after the seminar about a possible error being made in assessing learning difficulties, which I have written down, somewhere here." Dad pulled a card out of his wallet.

"I have it now, it's called 'Savant Psychopathy', which was being misdiagnosed as a major condition he called 'Autism'. The doctor said he thought Robbie may only have a learning difficulty that can be addressed with patience and a special education program, and later in life, may even develop skills beyond the average."

"That sounds great, Dad. So Robbie will be able to go to the school and still live here," Lettie declared, encouraged like me about Robbie's future.

"It's not that far to Peaceful Creek."

"There's two problems, Lettie. One is that the police have to allow Robbie to leave the asylum, and that depends on the director of the asylum agreeing with the assessment of Dr Lesser, the second is, for Robbie to improve quickly he needs to live at the Special School until he is at least twenty."

"So, how come Robbie's home now, if he's not allowed to leave the asylum. Doesn't make sense to me?" I asked, confused by the inconsistency of the people in charge of Robbie.

"Apparently, it's something they always do at Easter and Christmas. Robbie has to be back at Annadale before five on Monday afternoon. So, all we can do is wait for Dr Lesser," Dad explained, with a fair degree of resignation in his voice.

"Well, he's here now. So, I'm gonna make the most of it. If he wants to read, I'll read with him, if he wants to go for a walk, I'll go with him. And I haven't heard him sing before, that's something new," I stated, trying to inject some enthusiasm into the discussion.

Soon conversation turned away from Robbie to events around the farm, the local comings and goings, and even Aunty May's possible romance with the foreman. The catch-up continued until the wee hours of the morning but eventually the yawns told us we were done for the night and it was time to pull up stumps.

*

Saturday turned out to be somewhat of a wasted day with rain coming in sideways from the west, pushed by a gale force wind, ruining Mum's plan for a leisurely picnic by the river. Everyone, except Robbie, ending up around the kitchen table playing cards, spinning yarns, and telling some of the funniest jokes I'd ever heard.

Lettie and I took it in turns to tell watered down versions of some of the weird incidents that led to Lettie getting the job in Madeline's kitchen, while polishing off cuppa after cuppa, as well as the cakes and sandwiches that Mum and Lettie had got up early to prepare. This was as hard as the day was going to get.

Sunday morning, I helped Tiny move some of the sheep he and Dad had been bringing up to condition into another paddock, and some other odd jobs around the farm, while Dad took Mum into town to go to church. Dad still refused to go inside with her, blaming what happened to his brother in the Great War on all the Christian faiths, who he said did nothing to stop the catastrophe.

Mum and Lettie prepared a beautiful roast chicken lunch, so we used it as another fair excuse to loll away the afternoon by eating and drinking too much, while telling the same yarns that had already been trotted out the day before.

After we had our fill of lunch, Dad told Robbie he could leave the room to study if he wanted. Robbie didn't need to be told twice, and was off like a shot. When Robbie was safely in his room, Dad said he wanted to say something to the family before we cleared the table, and then waited patiently for our full attention.

"It's been a tough couple of months for all of us, that's one thing we can agree on, so I think it would be clearly remiss of me, if I didn't say something in the way of an apology for making things harder on everybody, than they needed to be," Dad said faltering for a moment before continuing.

"Setting fire to my truck was the stupidest, stupidest thing I have ever done," his bottom lip started to quiver as he looked away from us.

"Dad, you don't have to. Everything's all right now, isn't it?" Lettie asked and then looked at me to see if I knew more.

"No, nothing else can go wrong, Lettie," Dad replied, barely holding himself together. "Just let me finish. I want to say sorry to you all."

"Edwin, Leticia's right. You don't have to apologise," Mum jumped in. She was not known to say a lot, so when she speaks, everyone listens. "We know you only did it for Robert. He will get into Peaceful Creek, I firmly believe that. And, I also believe Dr Lesser has Robert's best interests at heart. I've held my tongue for long enough, but now I have something to say." Mum looked at Tiny, Lettie and then me, in order.

"Leticia, you've been given a wonderful opportunity at the King's College — so, stay there. Vernon and Sebastian, you both have jobs, many don't. Look after what you've got. Also, Robert is your dad's and my responsibility. So, let us put our house in order, our way."

Everyone was stunned into silence to hear Mum speak this way.

"Righto, I've told everyone off now, so you kids can get up and do the dishes if that isn't too much to ask. Dad and I have things we need to discuss."

All three of us not-quite-so-grown-up kids got up and quietly cleared the table and then toddled off to the kitchen. We had been told, without any doubt, that the folks would ask for our help, if, and when they needed it, and not before.

Later on Sunday night at supper, everyone had a good

laugh about how serious Mum had been in the afternoon. Lettie and I joked about how she had made us feel like we were ten again. But, Mum had made her expectations clear, she wanted us to act like the adults we had become.

Robbie came out of his room after supper wanting Lettie and I to sing the sea shanty 'Botany Bay' with him before we went back to the city tomorrow. We were a hilarious musical act singing all the wrong words completely out of tune around the piano; the perfect note to end our last night at home.

*

The next morning, we reluctantly left the farm to catch the train back to the city. Lettie and I said our goodbyes to Mum, Dad and Robbie at home, telling them that everything would turn out fine with Dr Lesser's help, and that we would write more often, instead of leaving it up to Aunty May to relay our news.

Tiny took us to the train station, carrying Lettie's canvas bag onto the platform, before saying: "I've been thinking about coming down to the city myself, if ya don't mind a visitor. After all, Aunty May keeps asking me to come and stay, in every one of her letters," Tiny said.

Lettie and I winked at each other and said that we'd

come across some places in town during the last four weeks that would scare the pants off him.

Tiny replied that nothing in the city could ever scare him, but I guaranteed him he wouldn't say that, if he had seen the display a set of twins put on at the 'Red Square'.

"Or some students at a university debate," Lettie added.

Lettie and I talked our heads off, all the way back to the city, excited and positive about Robbie and the brighter prospects back home.

As we stepped from our carriage on the 'Spirit' onto the packed platform of Spencer Street Station, washed-out from our trip, the first person we noticed, stood head and shoulders above the rest.

It was Charlie, looking down in the mouth.

This wasn't a complete surprise, although Lettie and I expected Charlie or Elaine would come around a little bit later after we returned to let us know that William had gone, and maybe ask us the awkward question; if we knew he was leaving, or where he was going.

Lettie and I hated lying to anyone, especially people we really cared about, like Elaine and Charlie, but we couldn't see any way around this without telling a white lie; if only for the sake of not making William's leaving any harder than it was.

"Charlie, how ya doing? You didn't have to come and meet me at the station," Lettie shouted as Charlie approached, slightly overdoing it.

"I'll be seein' ya tomorra' at the uni."

"I've got some news for ya both," Charlie murmured, preparing us for what we knew was coming. "I think it's bad news, but anyway. William has left for Spain. He says he's not going there to fight, though he would not ease our minds beyond that. He says he will return to Elaine, and us, of course."

"This is terrible, Charlie. How is Elaine? She must be beside herself with worry," said Lettie quietly.

"She found out Friday morning, in a letter William left under her door. She cried for the next two days but she was better yesterday, and today. Now she seems resigned to it, even angry at him. I think it would be for the best, Lettie, if you could wait for a day or so, before going to see Elaine. She's not returning to lectures until Wednesday."

Charlie stopped, and then shook his head. "I just don't know what's got into him. Maybe, he wants to see things firsthand, that's all I can think of … sorry for hitting you with news like this as soon as you step off the train, but I felt you should hear it from a friend."

"Thanks, Charlie," I replied. "It's hard to understand why he would want to go to Spain when he has so much to stay here for. I just hope he does what he has to do and then comes back quickly, in one piece."

"We all do, Charlie," Lettie added. "I'll go and see Elaine later in the week, she may feel better by then. I just wish

William could have thought about ..." Lettie's voice faded as she looked down at the ground.

"I'll leave you to get back to your aunt's," Charlie mumbled to himself, appearing done in. "Sorry again for ruining your return."

"No, you haven't Charlie, not at all," I insisted before shaking his hand.

"Thanks for coming down to let us know," Lettie said and then gave him a peck on the cheek, before saying we would stay in touch.

Charlie headed quickly toward the front of the station, Lettie and I followed slowly behind.

12

'Coming of Age'

There were three loud knocks on my flyscreen door, and then, "Grub, are ya there?"

It was Lettie calling out to me from just outside my digs, late Saturday afternoon.

"Yeah, Lett," I replied casually. "What d'ya want?"

"Can ya come downstairs, straight away? I have someone I'd like ya to meet." And then after a second, "And be on ya best behaviour," she said giving the screen door a small whack as she left.

I jumped off my bed, the only thing I could think of was that Lettie's new beau must have dropped in to meet Aunty May and me.

Bugger! I'm probably too late to see the look on Aunty May's face when she first notices the age of this fella.

I was glad for this diversion though, little had happened in almost a month since our return to the city after Easter, little except the news of Madeline's husband, Leo clearing out.

Two weeks after Easter, Madeline found a note after work on her kitchen table, hastily written by her husband, stating that he was going back to Queensland for work, but no mention of when, or if, he might be returning.

I told Lettie it was no surprise to me that he would do something like that to Madeline. Lettie said Bernadette was heartbroken that he had gone.

*

"Look, Sebastian! Leticia has brought a man around for us to meet," Aunty May announced, stating the obvious as I walked in through the screen door of her kitchen, to see Lettie standing next to the communal table, holding tightly onto the right arm of the older man she had danced with at the Parmenter's soirée.

I looked him up and down as he stood tall and confident next to Lettie and realised his older-than-thirty-years appearance had more to do with his receding hairline than to any other obvious signs of aging. I was relieved that he wasn't overly dandy, looking relaxed in a light grey suit, and a green Windsor knot tie hanging long over a brand new white shirt.

"Pleased to meet you ..." I began, before the man jumped in.

"Call me, Walter ... Walter O'Neill," he said and then leant forward to shake my hand. I half expected to hear an Irish accent with a name like O'Neill, but to the contrary he had a faint hint of an English one.

"Are you originally from Melbourne, Walter?" I asked, trying to pin down his accent.

"No, I grew up in Newcastle, my parents are still there. I've been down in Melbourne for over ten years though, so only ten years to go before I become a local."

Against my will, I was already taking a liking to this fellow, and as I watched Lettie whisper something in his ear, I knew it was only a matter of time before Walter became everything in her life.

"Walter is taking Leticia out for a walk around Carlton Gardens this afternoon, Sebastian, but I insisted they have a cup of tea first, so we can get to know Walter better," Aunty May declared, while turning to look directly at me, as if she wanted me to keep asking questions.

"Well, sit down then."

Aunty May went to grab the teapot while Lettie sat down next to Walter on the far side of the table. I sat down next to Aunty May's seat on the near side, facing them, as if it was a real interrogation.

"Seb, Walter works on the docks in Port Melbourne as a welder, but he would love to be a painter if he could, like in portraits, you know," Lettie said somewhat proudly, though it was always a little strange to hear Lettie call me Seb, instead of Grub.

"On the docks, hey?" I returned. "I hear it gets a bit willing down there at times. Must be difficult to keep yourself out of trouble?"

"It's not easy, Seb," Walter replied while sitting forward. "Hardly a day goes by when you don't see someone pinned up against a wall. You have to keep your wits about you."

"Did I hear someone mention portraits before," Aunty May asked as she returned to the communal table with her favourite silver teapot. "I love the fine arts."

"Walter is a portrait painter, Aunty. He is taking me to see the Autumn Exhibition at the Artists' Society next weekend, just before your birthday, Seb," said Lettie giving me a wink.

"If that's all right with you, May," Walter added.

"I may like to see the exhibition myself, Walter. If I'm not in the way," Aunty May hinted. "Is there a featured artist this season?"

"A small gallery will have selected works from the Heidelberg School," Walter replied, his eyes lighting up. "Impressionist works are my favourite, May. They give so much depth to a tableau."

"I think the Impressionists are taking the easy way out, Walter. I like the subject to look just the way it does in real life," Aunty May argued, sticking her nose up in the air.

Walter and Aunty May then began discussing the merit, or lack of, of almost ever style of portraiture known to man, while Lettie and I made faces at each other like we used to when we were kids. Eventually, Lettie had to step in.

"It's starting to cloud over outside, Aunty. So, perhaps Walter and I should go for our walk now while we still can."

Everyone around the table got up, and then Walter thanked Aunty May for the tea and welcoming him into her home.

"May, I insist that you accompany Lettie and me to the Autumn Exhibition, and if we are there at the right time, the Society's resident opera students will be performing in the main gallery."

"It will be a pleasure to accompany you and Leticia," Aunty May acknowledged. "It is so nice to meet a man that thinks for himself."

This was huge compliment, and didn't go unnoticed by Lettie. I joked to Walter as he held open the screen door to allow Lettie to go through that I'd been thinking of going to an art exhibition myself for quite a while, which he discreetly shook his head to, before firmly shaking my hand on leaving.

By the time Lettie and Walter had left, I had completely forgotten about the age difference between the art-loving dock worker and my kid sister.

*

I had tested the water during late April to see if it was safe to return to my original way home from work through the Magenta Push's stomping ground. I figured that after two months all should be forgiven regarding my incident with the Pom and his little Irish mate. Although, I didn't expect to be given a pat on the back from the owner for starting the ball rolling that got rid of them.

I was fifty yards from Lygon Street, trudging along Queensberry on Friday afternoon at the end of another heavy day of work, when I saw a young woman in a bright pink polka dot dress, fluffing up her bouffant blonde hair whilst leaning against a brick wall near the front of a long porch that led to what I believed to be the rear of the Magenta Club.

I nodded to this woman who continued to stare at me while taking a slow drag through her extended cigarette holder, blowing out a small cloud of smoke without returning my welcome.

I passed the porch, not thinking anything of her lack of response, when suddenly I heard a squawking voice call out from behind me.

"You're Sebastian, aren't you ... William's friend?"

I turned around to see the young woman's pale, overly made-up face, sticking out from around the porch, onto the footpath of Queensberry Street.

"Yeah," I replied without much thought, then realising she may have news of William, walked rapidly back towards her.

"Have you heard from William?" I asked, anticipating that she had.

"Nuh!" she gratingly replied "But, I was told to pass on a message from someone else if I ever saw you again."

Again! I've never seen her before in my life.

"From whom?" I asked studying her to see if I recognised her from somewhere.

"From Clarisse, she wanted me to pass on that she has been moved to Sydney by Madam Mayer. And that she is happy to go there, and not to be concerned for her." The woman stopped, then walked out onto the footpath in front of me, stating: "You don't know who I am, do you?"

I was already taken aback by the mention of Clarisse, but for the life of me I didn't know who this woman was.

"Clarisse appreciated your discretion at the Parmenter's soirée. It was for the best, not to make a scene," the working girl declared, still staring at me, before taking another drag of her cigarette.

This woman wasn't the redhead; she wasn't tall enough, so she had to be the dark-haired girl standing next to Clarisse at the soirée.

"That was a great night. Do you know if Madam Mayer is going to let Clarisse do her nurse training in Sydney?" I asked, hoping she would be given a way out of the trade.

"You know she won't, Sebastian. A volunteer is the best she can hope for. None of us are allowed to dream."

"Thanks for passing on the news about Clarisse. I have lost a bit of contact with Elaine and Charlie since William left for Spain," I explained, grateful in a way to have run into this woman. "I don't even know how the Aid stands are goin'..."

"They're going well. I like doing them, it's better than

hanging around here. I've had to do a few extra since Clarisse and William left, though," the young woman said and then almost laughed, which had me bemused.

"You were really calm when William yelled at you in Emerald Hill, Sebastian. A lot of blokes would have jacked up at that."

I was gobsmacked by what she had just said. It now hit me that I had seen this woman before, probably many times; she was the assistant I never spoke, or paid much attention to at the Emerald Hill Aid for Spain stand.

She was right in front of my eyes and I didn't even notice her.

"You were so naïve when I first saw you on Queensberry, it makes me laugh to think back. You have grown up so much since then. Sebastian, I have to go inside, and I better not be late, Madam has already had a few moments today." The woman smiled, and then something seemed to cross her mind.

"Can you do me a huge favour, Sebastian?"

"Sure ..." I replied cautiously. "If I can."

"Clarisse told me not to forget to let one of her best friends know she was going, but he's always stuck in his projection room," she said as if someone was hurrying her. "I'd love to go up to his room like William used to, but those steep stairs scare the hell out of me." She then looked back at the silver sheet-metal door at the end of the porch, as if she expected it to open any second.

"You're talkin' about Sidney, aren't ya?"

"Course. You know, he even told Clarisse that one day he would make an honest woman out of her."

Sidney, you old dog!

I would go and tell Sidney tomorrow that Clarisse had gone, but how could a girl not much older than Lettie think that all her dreams were over.

"What's all this crap about not being able to dream? You can do whatever you want," I told her as she stepped back up onto the porch.

"You wouldn't say that if you were born a girl, Sebastian?" the young woman scoffed. "There's not too many choices if you don't get married. And don't tell me you like throwing sheepskins around all day."

"Tell ya what, what if ..." It wasn't clear in my mind what I was about to ask, but I had to wait as a big bruiser of a man in a black suit and bowler hat started shouting from the silver sheet-metal door.

"Daphne, get your skinny arse in here. Madam wants ya, now."

"Are ya workin' tomorra' afternoon?" I asked quickly, trying not to get her into trouble.

"Nuh ... Why?" Daphne looked at me puzzled.

"I said get your arse in here Daphne before I come out and kick it," the large man snarled.

"Can you give us one minute, mate? I just want to ask her a question," I yelled back, not believing his rudeness.

"You can talk to the stupid slut all you want if you go around the front and hand over some coin, you drongo."

"What did you call her, you friggin' baboon," I shouted stepping up onto the porch as the foul-mouthed thug slammed shut the sheet-metal door behind him.

"Don't get involved, you little turd. I'll wipe the floor with ya. She's not worth it."

Daphne grabbed me by the arm dragging me from the porch, telling me he was right, and I had no place in their world, at the same time as Madam Mayer opened the rear door to the Magenta Club, taking a step outside, and then stopping suddenly as she realised we were in the middle of something.

"What's happening, Daphne?" Madam Mayer asked a lot quieter than I expected. "Is everything all right here?"

"I'm coming in, Madam," Daphne replied just as quietly. "I ran into Sebastian. You remember his sister Lettie from the Parmenter's soirée?"

Madam Mayer looked at me as if I wasn't even there, and then said, "Come in now, Daphne."

I stepped up onto the porch to show support to Daphne, not trusting my large friend or Madam. Daphne turned her face to me and whispered, "Regent" softly, before turning back to walk past the massive member of the Push, who stood arms crossed in front of me.

The big thug then turned and yelled "Slut" into Daphne's ear, making her cower. As he turned his face back to me, I struck him to the left of his jaw with as much force as I could muster, but with little effect, only seconds later his huge right fist smashed into my ribs.

I hit the wall of the porch, and then dropped down onto the deck, as a kick to the same spot followed shortly afterwards. I felt myself drifting out of consciousness as I saw the thug step back to kick again.

I could feel myself being dragged, it seemed like only seconds later, when I heard a familiar voice.

"Now listen you half-wits, I want you to put him down ... gentle."

"Piss off, you old bastard. This is none of your business," said the large man that had hit me as I was dropped onto a hard surface.

I sat up slowly, and then gradually became aware that I was on the Queensberry Street footpath near my foreman, his right hand stuck deeply inside his Gladstone bag, standing toe to toe on the porch with two of the Magenta Push boys; Daphne and Madam Mayer nowhere to be seen.

My foreman then said quietly as the thug that I had not seen before went to step behind him.

"Please, don't do that, mate, I sharpened the fleshing knife in my hand before I left work."

The monster of a man stopped dead in his tracks, not prepared to take a chance.

"I've seen you stupid bastards pushing people around here for years, and I'm not the only one fed up with it," my foreman snarled and then started pushing them backward along the porch.

"Sebastian and I are going home for tea, and if I so much as hear of any one of you pieces of shit, mistreating anybody, especially your girls, I will pick you off, one by bloody one, and leave your friggin' ears stuck to this shiny, little door here. Is that clear enough for your thickheads?" the foreman shouted.

The two members of the Push hesitated, they didn't want to be shown up in front of the small crowd that had gathered, and I'm sure they would have had blades on them, but when knives come out, things take a serious turn. They stepped back to the silver sheet-metal door, unsure of, but not prepared to play my foreman's bluff.

I had managed to stand myself up, feeling massive pain with every movement while my foreman stepped slowly back to the edge of the porch and then lowered himself onto the footpath.

No-one said a word to us as we left.

I leant on my foreman's shoulder for the short, but painful walk back to Aunty May's, stopping before we entered the lane that led to the rear door of our doss house.

"You're a bloody fool, Carmichael, why do you keep getting mixed up with those mugs?" the foreman scowled but still held down his voice. "Now, we've gotta keep a lid on this, your aunt doesn't need to know about any knife play ... so as far as I'm concerned, this was an accident at work — right!"

"Sorry," I replied, nodding my acceptance to the foreman, "but I thought the bloke in the bowler hat was gonna hit one of the girls."

"You can't save the world, Seb, and I couldn't have saved either of us if they had known I only had a small apple pairing knife in my hand," the foreman announced and then laughed to himself before we headed into the lane.

I think that was the first time my foreman had called me Seb.

*

When I woke up, my tiny room was full of sunlight and I could hear a loud ringing sound in my ears. It took me nearly a minute to figure out what day it was and then another to remember the mess I had caused yesterday. I went to move, but the whole left side of my body was stiff and numb, and when I forced myself to sit up, I felt a massive stabbing pain around where my left ribs should be.

I laid back again and made myself as comfortable as possible, realising too late that I shouldn't have tried to be a hero and in the process probably made Daphne's life a whole lot harder than it already was.

What the hell was I thinking?

Although, one thing I will never regret is hitting that bastard that abused her. He deserved it and a lot more than I could deliver. I should have stepped back and thought it through, there's more than one way to fix people like him up, and I was just lucky my foreman came along at the right time, and decided to help me out.

William had said that the owner of the Magenta Club in Sydney was a strong supporter of the Spanish Aid Committee, and although Clarisse may be telling him what's happening in Melbourne, a few phone calls from committee members down here would make him stand up and take a lot more notice, because there is one thing I have learned over my time: bullies never stop, until someone decides to stop them.

I don't like doing it, being a dobber, but as soon as I was able to I planned to talk to Elaine and tell her about the treatment the girls she works with every weekend on the Aid for Spain stands are receiving from the likes of Madam Mayer, and ask if she could pass that on to her mum and dad, and the Aid committee, who I am sure would not be very happy at all.

It came back to me just then that Lettie and Walter were taking Aunty May to the Artists' Society this afternoon, and I hoped it was going well, but what I didn't know was if my foreman had told anyone about my being 'injured at work', or if he was keeping a complete lid on the whole horrible business.

Yesterday, Daphne said "Regent" as she passed me on the porch at the rear of the Magenta Club, and I would have bet my life on the fact that she wanted me to meet her at the Regent Theatre today, so we could go and see Sidney together, high up in his projection room, which was pretty much the same thing that I was about to ask her, before the trouble began.

I could really do without climbing up the steep stairs at the rear of the projection room at the moment, because I wasn't even sure if I could get out of bed, let alone make it to the Regent, and then find Daphne, with the rarest of possibilities that Madam Mayer would allow her to leave the Club after what had happened yesterday.

But as long as there was a slim chance Daphne might show up, I had to prove to her that she was worth it.

*

It took me over an hour to walk from Aunty May's to the Regent Theatre, and then I waited for another hour in front of the brilliantly lit foyer, before finally admitting that Daphne wasn't going to show, or wasn't permitted to; or perhaps I had got it all wrong in the first place.

It was disappointing because it could have been quite a lot of fun going back to see Sidney again, with someone who had never seen his amazing little world before. But see Sidney I had to, because someone had to let him know about Clarisse leaving.

I got the painful part of climbing up the steep stairs over quickly, basically using the right side of my body to pull myself up, before receiving a warm welcome from Sidney and a comfortable place to sit to watch the last of *Lloyds of London*; it was good to be back.

After Sidney had wound down his projector until the evening session, I told him about Clarisse being sent to Sydney, and what had happened recently.

"I knew Clarisse wasn't happy with Madam, but I didn't know how nasty she had become. And I can't believe she didn't do anything to stop her thug beating into you?" Sidney stated, seeing anger in him for the first time.

"Didn't have time, Sidney, it was all over in seconds," I grinned. "I'm no prize-fighter."

"No, I can see that, Seb, but it shouldn't have happened, and young Daphne works so hard on the Aid stands," Sidney added shaking his head.

"I am going to Sydney in a few weeks to look at a new style 35 mm projector that the owners want to buy, so while I'm there I will go and see Clarisse, and Isaiah, the owner of the Club, who I have met once before at an Aid committee meeting, and I will have a few strong words with him about Melbourne."

"It's a shame it had to come to this," I asserted, but knew I should lighten the subject up.

"And, how are you going yourself at the moment, Sidney. Still tied to the projector?"

"Can't get away from it, flat out like a lizard, I think

is the expression," Sidney replied, and then laughed out loud, which was good to hear.

"I think my job is the only one not affected by the Depression, in fact, every theatre owner is crying on my shoulder at the moment that they want projectionists. You should give it a go yourself, Seb. I think you would like it," Sidney announced, looking like he was fair dinkum.

"I don't know, Sidney. I only just scraped through the Merit Certificate and these machines look so technical," I admitted.

"Well give it some thought, because I have thought of asking you, ever since you came up here with William. And as for Bill, I would have thought he could send us a letter or something by now," Sidney wondered. "You know about Agatha, don't you?"

"Yes," I nodded. "I think he made a very brave choice to go and help her."

"I do too," Sidney agreed.

"All right, Seb, I'm a busy man. Do you want me to teach you to become a projectionist ... Yes or no?"

I sat looking at Sidney, not believing that I was being asked to decide my whole future in a few seconds, but maybe that's the way life works.

"Yes," I replied loudly, the sound filling our tiny room, as I felt an amazing sense of relief that I had finally done something right for myself. "But, can you train me at the weekends for a start until I can get my family and my foreman used to the idea? I owe them a lot."

"Fine, what if we begin next Saturday afternoon, just for a couple of hours. I'm sure you don't want to climb up the stairs again tomorrow."

"Too right, I don't," I acknowledged, "and thanks a lot for doing this for me, Sidney."

I could have sworn that the pain in my ribs had decreased by half as I walked a little faster back to Aunty May's, excited, but also scared that one day I will be responsible for making a film run as smooth as silk, in a theatre where the owner would be taking a huge risk on a very nervous, newly trained projectionist.

*

Lettie brought two people home from work with her on Wednesday afternoon and a cake from Madeline. Elaine and Charlie were extremely cheerful as they were asked to come into Aunty May's kitchen, and it had little to do with my twenty-first birthday.

Elaine and Charlie introduced themselves to Aunty May. They chatted for ages before Elaine revealed she had finally received a letter from William, and to her everything in it sounded positive.

"William wrote that he was due to meet Agatha in Barcelona a few days after this letter was sent, and that she had sent him a note stating she wanted to leave Spain for a rest in France or England. But, William didn't say if he was planning to stay with her the whole time or if he was coming back home."

"Reading between the lines, it sounds as if Agatha is exhausted and if she has a long enough break, she will find it difficult to return to Spain," Charlie assumed, I think for Elaine's benefit.

"We can only hope so, Charlie," Elaine quietly accepted. "Now, it is Seb's birthday. It should be about him."

"No, Elaine, that's the best present I could have hoped for. And did I hear someone mention that they had brought around a bottle of beer to share?" I said looking at Charlie who immediately pulled out a bottle from an inner pocket of his coat.

In the lane at the rear of Aunty May's, Charlie poured a glass of beer for each of our small group of friends, and then he, Lettie and Elaine shouted.

"Happy birthday, Seb. Cheers!"

We all had a swig and then I called for another toast.

"And, here's to absent friends," I said as we raised our glasses again, before drinking the last of our beer.

*

A light drizzle had turned to steady rain, soaking my gabardine coat, as I pushed my way through the thick ivy that still choked the path that led to the rear of Madeline's house, glad to see a light on and movement through the small glass window in the door.

I knocked firmly on the same fly-screen door that I had passed through on more than one occasion of need.

"Is that you, Sebastian?" Madeline shouted above the steady beating sound of the rain on her roof.

"Is everything all right?" she added, peering through the small window, probably wondering why anyone would be calling in this weather.

Madeline unlocked the door, and then held open the screen door while still holding her dressing gown tight around her waist.

"No, everything is fine, Madeline," I replied, shivering as I spoke.

"Just dropping in to say hello."

"Come on in out of the rain, Sebastian," Madeline demanded, with a little concern in her voice. "You look soaked, you duffer."

I stepped only a foot inside the door, apologising as a large puddle of water formed almost immediately.

Madeline told me to wait where I was, while she went to grab a towel.

"I came by because I wanted to tell you something ..." I started to yell, when I saw Bernadette wheel herself into the kitchen, looking excited, before stopping suddenly, perhaps thinking I was someone else.

"How are you, Bernadette?" I asked, glad that she was home.

"Pretty good, thanks, Sebastian," she returned in her tiny voice. "How are you?"

"Better on seeing you, Bernadette," I winked.

Bernadette smiled and then waved before she went back in the lounge and I was left wondering how anyone could have left such a beautiful child. Madeline returned seconds later, throwing me a towel.

"Madeline, I can't stay. I just wanted to thank you for the cake you sent me on my birthday."

"You're very welcome, but you shouldn't have gone out in the rain to tell me that," Madeline replied, looking a little perplexed.

"You might as well have a cup of tea while you are here," Madeline suggested. "Then, if you remember why you really dropped in, you can tell me."

"Madeline, what I came around for, is to tell you something that I should have told you on more than one occasion, and I didn't. And that is thank you for what you have done for Lettie, and me, when we really needed a friend. You changed our lives."

Madeline stepped up close and put her arms around me, and despite my wet clothes held me tightly, finally releasing me as she said.

"Thank you for saying that, Sebastian, I have been so unsure of myself since my husband left ... I am very grateful for your kind words." She pulled away and said, "Now, this puddle is getting bigger, and a little birdy told me that you might be making a career change, so you'd better get on with it."

I stopped a few yards from the back door and then turned back to Madeline.

"Madeline, why did you take me in on the night of the fight?"

"Because you reminded me of my youngest brother — and I miss him very much."

*   *   *

Post Script

On August 27, 1938, after receiving massive internal injuries when the supply truck he was driving in support of Republican forces was forced off the road during an air raid, William Albert Reinecke, weakened by exhaustion, passed away in a small Spanish village, less than thirty miles from the French border. Madeline's husband, Leo McFarlane himself badly wounded, lay by his side.

After receiving safe passage from the Provisional Government in Barcelona, Agatha Parmenter crossed the French border at Cerbère on February 12, 1939, only hours in advance of Franco's army.

A month later, Agatha attended a rally at Whitehall, London, at which she and another woman proceeded to 10 Downing Street, where they threw lambs' blood at the front door of the Prime Minister's residence, in protest at his betrayal of the Spanish Republic, as well as the men and women who came to its aid.

Glossary of slang terms

A bit for 'ron: A bit for later on

A bit of a hurry up: A hurry along, made to go faster

A bum: A person of poor character, often without means

A do: A show, event, party

A fair whack: A good slice, piece

A hiding: A beating

A lark: A lot of fun

A shag: Cormorant, often perched alone on a rock

A squiz: A quick look around

A zack: Sixpence, roughly five cents

Abode: Place of residence, home

Accept the cards as they were dealt: Accept what you have been given in life, your destiny

Adieu: French for goodbye, farewell

Aga: Cast iron stove and cooker

All and sundry: Everyone, the general public

All in a flap: To be agitated, panicky

All over the shop: Everywhere, all over the place

Anglophile: A person that loves everything English or British

ANZAC: Australian and New Zealand Army Corps

As happy as Larry: Extremely happy

As rare as hen's teeth: Very rare

Bag of fruit: A suit (clothing)

Baggy-green caps: Cap worn by Australian test cricketers

Battleaxe: A formidable, older woman

Beau: Boyfriend, male suitor

Be full of yourself: Exaggerated sense of self-worth

Be on the up and up: To be legitimate, honest or sincere

Be unable to lie straight in bed: To be too crooked or devious to lie straight in bed

Beggar belief: Too unbelievable to be credible

Beside oneself: Almost out of one's mind with a strong emotion, usually worry

Big bruiser: Big, powerful man

Big wigs: The people in charge, authority

Bite hard down the track: To have bad consequences in the future

Blowies: Blow or mature flies

Bludger: Useless character, often avoiding work or responsibility

Bluebaggers: Nickname for Carlton football club players (Australian Rules football)

Bodgey character: Worthless or untrustworthy character

Brothers in arms: Comrades in battle

Brouhaha: Noisy and over-excited reaction

Browned off, straight up: Very annoyed, straight away

Bugger: Bloke, man

Bulldogs: Nickname for Footscray football club players (Australian Rules football)

Bullshit: Lies, rubbish, crap

Busybody: A person who has to know everyone's business (see Sticky beak)

Buy for nicks: For next to nothing

Cackin' your pants: Pooing in your pants, scared

Camp rough: Sleep outdoors, often in a tent

Caper: Activity, game, line of work

Cat that got the cream: To be happy with what you've done

Cheshire cat smile: Broad smile; from the book 'Alice in Wonderland'

Chin wag: A chat, to talk to someone

Cinch: Easy

Clacker: Backside, bum

Clip under the ear: Slap behind the ear

Clobber: Clothes

Cockney: The accent of a native East Londoner

Cocky: Farmer, and or overconfident person

Coin: Money

Comeuppance: A punishment or fate that someone deserves

Connie: Tram or train conductor

Cop somebody: To hit somebody

Copper (the): Cylindrical tub for washing clothes in

Coppers: Police

Cottee's: Popular soft drinks at the time

Cotton on: Begin to follow the thread, understand

Couldn't knock the skin of a rice pudding: To have a
    punch too weak to do any damage

Crack up: Laugh hard or hysterically

Cut a pretty good rug: Dance really well, often
    energetically

Cylinders: Forerunner of the music disc

Dags: Dirty wool hanging off the back of sheep

Dandy: A man overly concerned with looking stylish

Dardanelles: Refers to WW1 military campaign (Gallipoli)

De rigueur: Standard practice, from French

Deadly: Extremely

Digs: Room, home

Dismissed offhand: To dismiss something without
    consideration

Do your 'nana': To lose your temper

Dob someone in: To inform, tell on someone

Dole out: Distribute, hand out

Doozy: Something outstanding, unique; origin
    Duesenberg luxury car of the 1920/30s

Dosh: Money

Doss house: Cheap lodging house

Down memory lane: To remember things in the past

Drab: Boring, dull, or lacking colour

Dray: A low, sturdy cart used for carrying heavy loads,
    generally pulled by a horse

Drink like it is going out of fashion: To drink large
    amounts in a short time

Drongo: An idiot, a fool. Named after a horse that never
    won a race

Duffer: A silly or inept person

Dummy: Open air seating at the front of a cable tram

Dungarees: Like overalls, but with a bib at the front held
    by straps over the shoulder

Dust up: Fight

Eejit: Irish slang for idiot

Evil eye: A look to inflict harm or suffering with a curse

Fair dinkum: Genuine, authentic

Fair touch up: A thrashing, soundly defeat

Famished: Hungry, starving

Fellmongers: Tannery workers who generally prepare
    sheepskins

Fellow travellers: A person who is sympathetic, but not a
    member of a certain group, or party

Fib: Small lie

Fine and dandy: Fine and well, everything as it should be

Fire and brimstone: The torments of Hell

Fix someone up: To get even with someone

Flat out like a lizard (drinking): To be very busy

Fleece someone: To steal money or goods by deceit

Fleshing knife: Long curved knife, sharpened on both
    sides

Flip your lid: Become angry, fly off in a rage

Folding stuff: Bank notes, money

For a song: Very cheaply

Franco: Leader of the Rebel Nationalist Army in Spain

Full of hot air: To talk without saying anything useful or
    with meaning

Galoot: Big, but perhaps not often bright man

Garb: Clothes of a distinctive style

Georges: Fancy department store in Melbourne, now
    defunct

Get on your bike: Get on your way, hurry

Get toey: On edge, ill at ease

Git: Not a smart person

Give someone stick: To tease or give someone a hard
    time

Glad rags: Clothes for a special occasion, Sunday best

Gladstone bag: Very popular working man's carry all at
    the time

Gorra hat: Spanish-style small hat

Gripe: To whine, whinge, complain

Gully trap: Trough with tap at the rear of a house, used
    frequently at the time

Gun the motor: Rev up the motor

Half-baked: Not quite right, or thought through

Hard earned: Hard earned money

Hard nuts: Tough guys

Haughty: Arrogantly superior, stuck up

Have a gawk: To stare or gape for no good reason

Have a run in with someone: To have a serious argument, or trouble with someone

Have a turn: To put on a performance by becoming unwell, or faint

Have a word with someone: To talk to someone in order to criticise them

Have some pull: Have an influence or say, to be able to pull strings

Have someone cold: To be exposed, to have no comeback

Have tickets on yourself: To have a high opinion of yourself

Having kittens: To be very nervous, or worried

Hay-making right: Wide sweeping punch with the right hand

Heidelberg School: Late 19th century impressionist art movement, based in Melbourne

Hell's bells: Said on surprise or anger, milder than 'bloody hell'

Hit a wall: To become suddenly exhausted, or sleepy

Hit the sack: Go to bed, go to sleep

Hostellerie: Lodgings (French)

Hotham Hill: Western area of North Melbourne (formally Hotham), almost obsolete usage

How many strips could somebody possibly tear off: How big a telling off could somebody get

I'm in suspenders: I'm in suspense (pun)

Icing on the cake: To finish something off nicely

Impressionist movement: Artists that capture an image as a glance, often painted outdoors

In the black: In credit, in the positive

Jack up: To rear up, to not take something well

Kerfuffle: Commotion or fuss

Kick oneself: To be angry at yourself

King hit: A sudden, powerful punch

Kip: A nap, short sleep

Knock down: Drink quickly

Knock off: To finish work for the day

Know the ins and outs: To know every detail

Kosher: Prepared according to Jewish custom, genuine

Lackey: Servant, flunkey

Lag on someone: To inform on someone (see Dob)

Lamb's fry: Fried lamb's liver

Lantern shows: Films shown in halls or smaller spaces using portable projectors

Larrikins: Boisterous, often badly behaved young men

Lash out: To spend freely on something Lay it on a bit thick: Grossly exaggerate something

Lazy wind: A wind too lazy to go around someone

Let someone go: To terminate employment, sack or fire someone

Like a shag on a rock: An isolated, exposed position

Little birdy: A person that is known, but not identified

Loll away: To relax, to lounge about

Long winded: To continue something over a prolonged
    period

Loo: Toilet

Loose cannon: An unpredictable person who could cause
    damage; from a loose cannon on a ship

Madam: A woman that runs a brothel, a female pimp

Majors: Goals (Australian Rules football)

Make a stand: To stop and fight for something

Manifesto: Publically declared aims

Mattock: Gardening hand tool, a cross between a pick
    and a hoe

Merit Certificate: Awarded at the end of Form 2 (current
    day Year 8)

Mick: Derogatory term for Irish people, or Roman
    Catholic

Milko: Milkman, delivering milk from behind a horse
    and cart

Moggy: House, or domestic cat

More crap than a night cart: Refers to a night cart that
    would routinely collect from lavatory pan

More front than Myers: Cheeky, bold person, not afraid
    to front up; from Myer, Melbourne

Muck up: To make a mess, bungle, spoil

Mug: Idiot or fool; also to rob people on the street

Natter: To talk casually

Nemesis: A long-standing rival, sworn enemy

No end of stick: No end of ribbing, constantly reminded

No qualms: No uneasiness or hesitation in doing
    something

Not know someone from Adam: To not know anything
    about a person

Off your own bat: Without assistance, independently;
    from cricket

Old biddy: Old woman

Old Dart: England

On the up: To be on the improve

Out of my league: To be out of reach, or unable to
    compete for something

Out of whack: Out of order, at the wrong time

Over the moon: Extremely happy, delighted

Pansy: Effeminate man or boy

Pay a pretty penny: To pay a lot

Phar Lap: Great Australian racehorse of the early 1930s;
    Maori for lightning

Pirouette: Turning on the spot, as in ballet

Pom: Common term for English people

Poppycock: To talk nonsense

Pork pie: Lie

Poser: Exhibitionist (see Show pony)

Prize Peacocks: Show-offs

Pro Bonos: Legal term for free or reduced fees for the
    public good; from Latin

Pugilist: Fighter/Boxer

Push: Common name for a street gang prior to World
War Two

Put on the books: To get a job, usually permanent

Quid: Pound sterling

Raw nerve: To touch on a sensitive subject

Ripper: Very good

Rolly: A cigarette rolled by yourself

Roomy: A boarder

Royboys: Nickname for Fitzroy football club players
(Australian Rules football)

Ruffle the feathers: To annoy or upset

Save your bacon: To save yourself from injury or harm

Scam: A dishonest scheme, a swindle

School of drinkers: Group of drinkers that buy (shout)
each other drinks

Scrapper: Street fighter

Scream blue-murder: Scream wildly, as if being attacked

Settle a score: To get even or back at somebody

Shenanigans: Spirited fun and games, from Irish slang

Sheilas: Girls

Shifty bugger: Sly or cunning person

Shirkers: People who dodge or avoid work

Shoot through: To clear or take off

Shoot: Polite version of shit

Show a stiff upper lip: To be steady and determined
in the face of danger; often in reference to English
people

Show pony: Flamboyant person who loves to be the
   centre of attention

Shyster: Underhanded or unscrupulous person

Silver screen: Cinema industry; taken from the colour of
   the screens in early cinema

Skulduggery: Dishonest activity or behaviour

Splash out: To spend freely

Slouch hat: Australian army hat with the left side of the
   brim turned up

Smarmy: Smart-mouthed, smug, insincere

Smart-aleck: An irritating person that thinks they know
   everything

Smidge: A very small amount

Smoko: Morning or afternoon tea

Snoop: To pry, look into other people's business

Soirée: An evening party, typically in a private house, for
   conversation and music; from French

Stick that in your pipe (and smoke it): Fun way of saying,
   you have to believe me

Stickybeak: To stick your nose in where it's not wanted

Stitch someone up: To make someone appear
   responsible when they're not

Strewth: From God's truth, to express mild surprise

Struggletown: Referring to Richmond in Melbourne,
   poor working class area at the time

Swell: Good

Tableau: Painting, from French

Tackers: Young children

Tad: A small amount or go to a small extent

Take something to heart: To take something over personally or seriously

Tan their hides: Spank their behinds

Tanked: Drunk

Tee up: To arrange something for somebody

Test the water: Try something before committing

The Big Smoke: A big city like Melbourne or Sydney

The Children's: The Children's Hospital

The flicks: Cinema, movies, or pictures

The good oil: A good piece of advice

The Hun: German soldiers, from WW1

The Irish rising in me: The anger rising in me

The Jive: Popular dance style in the late 1930s

The matinée show: The early show

The safe: Refers to Coolgardie safe, box cooled by evaporation

Third wheel: Someone not required, getting in the way

Thread the spool: Thread film through a projector

Tiff: Small argument

To lead up the garden path: To lead with misleading or dubious information

Tomcatting: To chase females at night

Too right: Exclamation that means I agree

Toot: Toilet

Torched: To set fire to, especially in act of arson

Touched: Slightly mad, crazy

Trifle with someone: To not take someone seriously

Turf out: To throw out, chuck out

Turn the other cheek: To refrain from retaliating after
being attacked

Turncoat: Traitor

Twig: To work it out

Two bobs worth: Opinion or advice; two shillings' worth

Tykes: A small child, often cheeky

Uncalled for: A low act, unnecessary

Unsavoury type: Offensive, distasteful

Upstart: Overconfident, usually young person

Veldt: Field, Plains, from Afrikaner

Warts and all: Everything, including the imperfections

Wet behind the ears: Without experience, immature

White lie: Small lie, often used to avoid making things
worse

Whiz-bang: Excellent or great; from WW1 ordnance that
made a similar sound

Wigs: Lawyers, solicitors

Willing: Aggressive, willing to fight

Without further ado: Without fuss or delay

Wowsers: Straight-laced people, spoilsports

Yonks: A very long time

You don't know the half of it: You don't know how things
really are

www.ingramcontent.com/pod-product-compliance
Lightning Source LLC
Chambersburg PA
CBHW072358110726

47909CB00003B/738